"I can't run away now. It's better if he focuses on me instead of...whoever he might already be stalking."

Daniel swung away, paced the length of the kitchen then back, his expression dark. "You infuriated him today. He can't kid himself anymore that you're secretly grateful to him for having the guts to do what no one else will, that you'd throw yourself into his arms in gratitude if he revealed himself to you."

"I know," Lindsay said softly. Her fingernails bit into her palms.

"You saw one of the bodies. You think you know what he's capable of, but you don't," he said harshly. "*Monster* is the right word for him. Can you imagine finding yourself locked in a freezer? It's dark and hopeless and you get colder and colder until ice forms in your nostrils and eyes and lungs." He planted his hands on the table and bent forward, eyes dark and boring into hers. "How do you think he'd kill you, Lindsay, now that you've violated his worldview?"

THE HUNTING SEASON

USA TODAY Bestselling Author

JANICE KAY JOHNSON

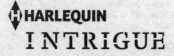

HARLEQUIN
INTRIGUE

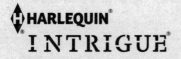

Recycling programs
for this product may
not exist in your area.

ISBN-13: 978-1-335-13649-7

The Hunting Season

Copyright © 2020 by Janice Kay Johnson

This edition published by arrangement with Harlequin Books S.A.

For questions and comments about the quality of this book,
please contact us at CustomerService@Harlequin.com.

Harlequin Enterprises ULC
22 Adelaide St. West, 40th Floor
Toronto, Ontario M5H 4E3, Canada
www.Harlequin.com

Printed in U.S.A.

An author of more than ninety books for children and adults with more than seventy-five for Harlequin, **Janice Kay Johnson** writes about love and family, and pens books of gripping romantic suspense. A *USA TODAY* bestselling author and an eight-time finalist for the Romance Writers of America RITA® Award, she won a RITA® Award in 2008. A former librarian, Janice raised two daughters in a small town north of Seattle, Washington.

Books by Janice Kay Johnson

Harlequin Intrigue

Hide the Child
Trusting the Sheriff
Within Range
Brace for Impact
The Hunting Season

Harlequin Superromance

A Hometown Boy
Anything for Her
Where It May Lead
From This Day On
One Frosty Night
More Than Neighbors
Because of a Girl
A Mother's Claim
Plain Refuge
Her Amish Protectors
The Hero's Redemption
Back Against the Wall

Brothers, Strangers

The Closer He Gets
The Baby He Wanted

The Mysteries of Angel Butte

Bringing Maddie Home
Everywhere She Goes
All a Man Is
Cop by Her Side
This Good Man

Visit the Author Profile page at Harlequin.com.

CAST OF CHARACTERS

Lindsay Engle—A Child Protective Services caseworker pursuing an investigation, Lindsay finds a murdered man, only the first of multiple killings. All the victims were abusive parents...and all were on Lindsay's caseload. Does the killer hate her...or does he believe he's giving her a gift by punishing people in a way she doesn't dare?

Daniel Deperro—A homicide detective trying to find a serial killer, Daniel isn't happy to be attracted to Lindsay when she's the obvious suspect. But the better he gets to know her, the more he fears *she* is the real focus of this killer.

Glenn Wilson—Lindsay's former boss, Glenn was Lindsay's mentor and biggest booster. Needing his support and friendship, she refuses to believe he could be a killer.

Matt Grudin—A fellow caseworker who didn't like being shut down romantically by Lindsay, he's antagonistic enough to make Daniel wonder to what lengths he'd go to ruin a woman he resents.

Ray Hammond—Another caseworker who'd once asked Lindsay out, Ray gives very mixed signals. How does he really feel about her?

Chapter One

Lindsay Engle set down the phone very carefully. If she'd given into her emotions, she'd have slammed it into the cradle and potentially shattered it.

The balding man who'd been chatting with another caseworker made his way between desks until he reached hers. Glenn Wilson, mentor and friend—and well able to read her, even when she was stone-faced. "What's wrong?" he asked her.

Quiet had stolen over the room, she realized. Glancing around, she saw that her coworkers' heads had all turned, too. She'd have sworn she hadn't raised her voice.

"I removed a boy from his home two weeks ago."

Nods all around; too often, as employees of Oregon State Child Protective Services, they had no choice.

"I placed him with his uncle, who sounded disgusted with his brother. Shane *liked* his uncle." Her jaw clenched so hard she wasn't sure she'd be able to relax it enough to say another word.

Glenn laid a hand on her shoulder. "Is the boy badly injured?" he asked, voice gruff but also gentle.

Lindsay shook her head, swallowed and said, "No, thank heavens. He collapsed trying to get on the school bus. The driver called 9-1-1, and Shane was transported to the hospital. That was the ER doc calling. Shane managed to tell them that his uncle Martin hurt him." More like beat him to within an inch of his life, from the sound of it.

She opened a desk drawer and took out her handbag. "I need to get to the hospital."

Ashley Sheldon, who sat behind the next desk, murmured, "That poor kid."

"Apparently, brutality runs in the family," Lindsay said bitterly.

"The cops arrest the creep?" Glenn asked.

"He's conveniently not home. I don't know whether he realized he'd gone too far, or whether he thought Shane would make an excuse and he'd skate."

"He fell down the stairs," suggested Matt Grudin, tone acid.

"Had a dirt bike accident," Ray Hammond, another coworker, added.

Dark humor was common in their profession, but all Lindsay could summon was a pathetic smile before she said, "I'm off."

As she walked away, behind her Glenn growled, "There's a reason I took early retirement."

She fully understood. Social workers, especially those on the front lines, burned out all too fast. Maybe she was getting to the point where she should do something else for a living. Something one step removed from children with purple bruises, black eyes and teeth knocked out by a fist, or girls who carried terrible secrets. How Glenn had stood it all those years, she couldn't imagine. She admired him and was grateful that since his retirement he still stopped by the office regularly to say hi and lend his support to anyone who was especially frustrated or down.

At the small community hospital, she went straight to the emergency room, where she was allowed in Shane's cubicle. As many times as she'd seen battered children and teenagers, she never got over the shock. His face was so swollen and discolored, she wouldn't have been able to recognize him as the boy who, despite his wariness, was still capable of offering an irresistibly merry smile.

Maybe she should say, *had* been capable.

The one eye he could open fastened on her. "Ms. Engle?"

At least, that's what she thought he'd said.

"Shane." At his bedside, she reached for his hand, but pulled hers back when she saw that his was heavily wrapped. "I'm so sorry. I never dreamed—"

"My fault," he mumbled through misshapen lips. "I thought—" He, too, broke off, but she had no trouble finishing the sentence. Shane had believed his uncle was a good guy.

"Can you tell me what happened? In ten words or less?"

The fourteen-year-old, tall for his age but skinny, tried to smile, then groaned.

Seized by guilt, Lindsay exclaimed, "I'm sorry! Forget it! We can wait until you don't hurt so much."

He gave his head the tiniest of shakes. "S'posed to clean the kitchen last night, and I didn't. He dragged me out of bed and…" He made an abortive gesture. "You know."

"I gather you talked to a police officer."

"Kinda."

"Okay. Did you have the MRI?"

She thought that was a nod.

"Has the doctor talked to you yet?"

"Waiting for you."

"Oh. Okay." She smoothed sandy blond, shaggy hair back from Shane's battered face. "You know this isn't your fault."

His face twisted slightly and one shoulder jerked in a shrug she had no trouble interpreting. Did Shane even believe the cruelty he'd lived through from his father was anything but normal? As with most abused children, he wouldn't have talked about it to his friends. For all he knew, the same crap might be going on behind closed doors in their homes. Now, having the uncle Shane had liked and trusted react so violently to his minor offense had to make him think men were always this violent…or else there was something about *him* that caused both his father and uncle to lose it.

Neither interpretation was healthy.

The original call regarding Shane had been referred to another caseworker, Emmett Harper. Emmett had thought Shane would respond better to a woman and transferred his case to Lindsay. Whether Emmett was right or not, Lindsay had never had any trouble with the boy, and thought he trusted her as much as he could trust anyone.

She hated that his ability to trust had taken another blow.

Lindsay hid a wince. Bad pun.

"*I* say it's not your fault," she told him, but saw his disbelief.

AN HOUR LATER, she'd talked to the doctor, a gray-haired, reassuring man who said Shane had suffered a concussion, two broken ribs, a broken cheekbone, three broken fingers, probably from blocking a punch, and a great deal of soft tissue damage. Nothing permanent, but he'd be in significant pain for weeks to months as the broken bones healed.

Shane was admitted for the night because of the head injuries, which gave Lindsay almost twenty-four hours to find him a new placement.

She also talked to the Sadler police officer who had responded to the call from the bus driver and who had driven to Martin Ramsey's house on the outskirts of town. They used a small room off the ER to talk.

"Shane says, after his uncle beat the crap out of him, he told him to take a shower and get ready for school. Sent the kid out the door to catch the bus."

"Did he really think nobody would notice Shane's face?" Lindsay said incredulously.

Middle-aged and seemingly steady, Officer Joe Capek shook his head. "If he did, he's delusional."

"Do you think he took off?"

Sounding doubtful, he said, "If he'd been afraid of trouble with authorities, he could have kept the kid home from school for a few days. Threatened Shane with what would happen if he told anyone."

Lindsay thought the same. "When do you plan to go back to the house?"

"I gather he works as a handyman?"

"More like he does remodels, but yes, he said he takes small jobs, too."

Capek shrugged. "Figured I'd try five thirty, before my shift ends."

"I'll meet you there," she said, rising to her feet.

"Is that smart?" he asked.

"I want to look him in the eye when you cuff him," she said grimly.

His mouth twitched into an almost smile. "Let's meet there, then."

By the time Lindsay drove to the old farmhouse on the outskirts of Sadler, a headache had begun climbing the back of her neck. She could feel the pitons being pounded in.

Unfortunately, Martin Ramsey did not appear to be home. As Officer Capek circled the house to knock on the back door, Lindsay peered into a dusty, small-paned window on the side of the outbuilding that appeared to serve as a garage. She spotted a lawn mower and a flatbed trailer, but no car or pickup truck.

They met back at their own vehicles.

"I can send a unit around later," he told her, and she nodded. Truthfully, there was no huge urgency to get their hands on Martin. He had no other children in the home who might be potential victims.

The next morning, she drove Shane to a receiving home, intended to be temporary. Late afternoon, she called Capek to learn he'd had a family emergency. Sadler was one of the larger towns in eastern Oregon, which meant only that it had a handful of traffic lights downtown and an array of essential businesses as well as a bunch of churches and taverns. The police department consisted of seventeen officers as well as a chief and captain. The resources weren't unlimited, and the county sheriff's department was stretched even thinner patrolling lonely miles of rural roads and highways. Lindsay had always found both agencies to be cooperative to the extent of their capabilities. This time, though, it appeared that in the absence of Officer Capek, nobody else had made any effort to catch up to Shane's uncle.

Too mad to wait, she decided to follow up herself. She wouldn't make contact, just check to see if there were indications the man was home. The situation was beginning to strike her as really strange. Had he gotten home yesterday evening and not wondered at Shane's absence? Or had he gotten nervous and gone to stay with a friend?

Or could he be at his brother's empty home? Austin Ramsey was serving a disgracefully short jail sentence for what he'd done to his son. Knowing that, Martin might have thought he could stay there for a week or two with no one the wiser.

Martin's own home first.

The aging house and barn and additional small outbuilding looked as deserted as they had yesterday. Even forlorn, Lindsay thought, although that was surely all in her head.

Disturbed, she turned her car around and went back out to the road.

Shane had grown up in a somewhat more modern rambler that was also set on two or three acres. As Lindsay turned into the long dirt driveway, she became uneasily aware that, without binoculars, the nearest neighbors wouldn't see what was happening here.

Her foot went to the brake. Maybe coming out here alone wasn't the smartest thing she'd ever done. But after a brief hesitation, she made sure the car doors were locked and went ahead. Why would he be a danger to her? He probably thought he was fully justified in punishing his nephew.

She rolled to a stop in front of the house, which at first sight showed no sign of life. Here, a double garage could be hiding his pickup truck.

Lindsay turned her Subaru Outback around, so that all she had to do was stomp down on the accelerator to escape. Then she leaned on the horn and watched the front door and windows through her rearview mirror.

Wait. Was that a light on inside?

Her internal debate was brief. This was hardly the first time she'd gone alone to speak to an abusive parent. Assaulting her wouldn't advance Martin's cause. To the contrary, in fact. He still technically had visitation with his own children, albeit they lived with their mother and a stepfather in Pennsylvania. Given his poor impulse control, it probably hadn't occurred to him that he had put that visitation in jeopardy by beating up his nephew.

Lindsay left the key in the ignition, her engine running and the driver side door open to facilitate a hasty escape. She wasn't even sure why she felt so tentative as she climbed the two porch steps and approached the front door.

Ringing the doorbell produced a sound inside she'd call a gong. When nothing happened, she eased toward the large front window. The blinds were down, but slanted to allow her to peer in. The interior was dim, but a light was definitely on deeper in the house. The kitchen?

She dialed 9-1-1 and clutched her phone in her hand with her finger poised over the screen as she left the porch and went around the house to the back. On the way, she reasoned with herself. Austin might well have left a light or two on in the house to make it appear someone was home. He could even have lights on timers. Lindsay didn't understand this instinct insisting that, all evidence to the contrary, someone was here.

The quiet seemed unnatural when the road wasn't that far away. She stopped in the middle of the overgrown lawn and looked around. Movement in the trees caught her eye, chilling her despite the heat of the day. She stared. She'd been imagining things; no one was there. A few leaves quivered, probably because a bird had taken off from that branch.

Taking a deep breath, she turned to the back stoop, which was just that: a concrete pad with a small extension of the roof sheltering it. She was only a few feet away, about to take a last look over her shoulder, when she saw that the door stood open by an inch or two.

She froze, eyes fixed on the thin band of light. Her finger twitched, but…what if she called the police, and it turned out Austin just hadn't latched the door when he left the house?

Somehow, Lindsay knew better and knew, too, that she was going to look inside. Her mouth was suddenly dry. She used her elbow to nudge the door. It swung silently inward, revealing a utility room with a bench for the owner to sit and remove boots. Two pairs had been neatly placed beneath the bench. Several coats hung on hooks on the wall. An empty plastic laundry basket sat atop the dryer. An open doorway led into the kitchen.

Lindsay tiptoed forward, straining to hear any faint sound. As she scanned the room, her nostrils flared at the sharp scent of something burning.

For a moment, she didn't understand why two feet clad in white athletic socks were in such an odd position. She took one more step as she grappled with the question…and saw a man sprawled on the kitchen floor. At the sight of his head and the blood pooling on the floor, her stomach lurched.

Dear God, he was dead. Murdered. And…he was at least the same general size and shape as Martin Ramsey.

DETECTIVE DANIEL DEPERRO groaned as the canned voice on his cell phone assured him he could go the company website and discover a wealth of information, freeing him from any necessity of bothering an actual person. He'd listened to the lengthy spiel and the ensuing elevator music six times now.

Since waiting on hold was a chronic time-waster for all detectives, he was mostly inured, but his mood hadn't been good today for no particular reason. His leg ached, although there was nothing new in that. When a high-caliber bullet shattered your femur, putting the pieces together was a little bit like trying to patch up poor Humpty Dumpty. And yeah, he hadn't enjoyed informing the parents of a high school senior that he had arrested their son for selling cocaine, and oh, by the way, the kid would stand trial as an adult since he'd turned eighteen three weeks before.

His desk phone rang and he picked it up, leaving his mobile phone on speaker so he wouldn't miss a single note of the music.

"Deperro."

"Detective, this is Officer Bowman. I just responded to a call from a CPS worker who found the man she was looking for dead. Head smashed like a jack-o'-lantern someone dropped. I don't see a weapon, but someone killed him."

"Address?"

Daniel committed the street address to memory and asked if the CPS worker was certain of the victim's identity. A murmur of conversation in the background was replaced by Bowman's voice.

"She thinks she knows who this is, but can't be positive."

"Okay. The name?"

Martin Ramsey rang some bells for him. Coming in to work yesterday, Daniel had taken note of the report of a severe beating given a fourteen-year-old boy and that the teen had tagged his uncle as the perpetrator.

Checking his computer, Daniel saw that an Austin Ramsey owned the home where the dead body had been found. Austin, however, was currently in the county jail. Interesting.

He grabbed his cell phone, cut off the beginning of the spiel, version seven, and walked out of the station to his car.

The drive didn't take ten minutes.

Somebody had filled potholes in the dirt driveway. Ahead, he saw a brick rambler with a double-car garage at one end. Two vehicles sat in front, one an SPD car with a rack of lights on top, the second a common crossover that would handle well in snow and ice, which they would certainly see plenty of this winter. In the crossover, he could see the back of a woman's head.

Officer Aaron Bowman came around the side of the house. He was young, twenty-eight or twenty-nine, and had impressed Daniel before with his steadiness and common sense.

When the two men met up, Daniel said, "That the caseworker?"

"Her name is Lindsay Engle. She took a boy named

Shane Ramsey from his father, who owns this place, and placed him with the uncle. According to her, a couple weeks later the uncle beat the boy bloody. Nobody has picked up the uncle yet, who apparently hasn't gone home. She thought he might be hiding out here."

"And that's who she thinks is dead in there."

"Yeah."

Daniel asked a few questions as the two men went to the back door, which according to the woman had been open. Bowman hadn't gone past the entrance between the utility room and the kitchen.

"Didn't need to check for a pulse," he said, his jaw tightening.

Daniel immediately saw why. Half the victim's head had been obliterated. He also understood Ms. Engle's doubts. If the dead man had any face left, it couldn't be seen from this angle.

The odd note was a small metal wastebasket sitting in the middle of the kitchen floor, only feet from the body. He took another step until he was able to see the burned, broken flakes inside, like blackened sheets of paper-thin, delicate phyllo bread.

Crumpled paper, he realized. A fire that had been deliberately set, and gone out when all fuel had been consumed.

Daniel called for CSI. He wanted to walk through the house, but found the front door locked and didn't want to contaminate the kitchen by tromping through it. He asked Officer Bowman to stay and to start a log of who came and went. Then he went to the caseworker's car and knocked on the passenger side window. She unlocked once he asked if he could get in to talk to her.

He turned in the seat to survey her, and felt an odd stirring he identified as surprise. In some inexplicable way, she didn't look like a Child Protective Services caseworker, yet he knew that was ridiculous. He'd worked with enough of her colleagues to be fully aware they could be young, middle-aged, near retirement, outwardly cheerful or glum, blue-eyed or brown. The stereotypes didn't work. About all he knew for sure was that in the local office, a majority of the caseworkers were women.

This one had medium brown hair worn in a roll on the back of her head, blue eyes and a voluptuous body he thought could be a problem when she worked with unstable men and hormone-ridden teenage boys. But that was none of his business.

What did make him curious was her guarded air. He wondered if she was ever completely open. The fact that he sensed she had secrets might in fact be his business.

"Ms. Engle?" He held out a hand.

Hers was icy cold. "That's right."

"Tell me what brought you here." He smiled, hoping to relax her. "Start at the beginning."

She spoke succinctly, her voice pleasingly husky. Mostly, what she told him was a recap. He listened intently when she explained her reasoning for checking out this house, and for deciding to get out of her car and ring the doorbell.

"You didn't consider calling for police backup?" he asked.

"I should have." Her cheeks warmed. "I don't like to do that unless I know something's wrong, though. I mean, that's a waste of your time. This was just…"

He waited through her hesitation.

Her eyes met his. "I really don't know. Just a feeling, I guess. I almost chickened out when I first came around the back of the house. I could have sworn someone was standing in that wooded area. But I don't know, when I kept looking I didn't see anyone."

Was she tossing out the possibility that someone else had been watching her to keep him from focusing on *her*? Or had a killer really been there, and she'd been an idiot to disregard what her instincts had surely been telling her?

She continued. "When I saw that the back door was open a crack, I justified going inside." She made a face. "I actually tiptoed, believe it or not."

Yeah, he could see her doing that. He wanted to say, *You know walking in that way was stupid, don't you?* Instead, he settled for an "uh-huh."

"What I don't understand is who could have killed him. It doesn't make sense."

She *sounded* sincere. Was she that good an actor? He must have hidden what he was thinking, because her expression didn't change until he asked, "Is Shane still in the hospital?"

Her mouth dropped open. "You're suggesting *Shane* would do this?"

"I'm asking where he is."

She didn't look very friendly now, but said, "I picked him up at the hospital late this morning and took him to a receiving home. I assure you, he's in no shape to borrow a bike, pedal across town and beat a man to death."

"But he has excellent motivation," Daniel said softly.

Her anger, or dislike, flared from a simmer to a rolling boil. "That's ridiculous! He never even fought back when his father abused him. He's a good kid. You might as well accuse me."

He didn't say a word, because yes, the thought had crossed his mind that she might have cracked and killed a man who epitomized everything she hated.

She retreated without moving a muscle. The rest of her answers were single syllables. He couldn't even blame her, but the reality was that he had to consider her a suspect at this point.

Ten minutes later, already on his phone, he watched her drive away. If she intended to call the receiving home, he'd beaten her to the punch—and what he learned in a brief conversation set a red flag to flapping.

Chapter Two

Shane was missing.

Lindsay learned as much when she reached the receiving home. Althea and Randy Price had never been among her favorite foster parents, but they'd seemed capable for short-term placements. Live and learn. Apparently Althea had shown Shane to his bedroom and then failed to notice his absence until four or five hours later.

The woman's round-cheeked face flushed. "I assumed he was sleeping."

Scared for Shane, Lindsay said, "You didn't check even once on a boy you knew had suffered a head injury and had spent the night at the hospital."

Randy Price glared at her.

Althea's chin rose defiantly. "You'll have to forgive me if I thought he needed sleep more than lunch!"

"He needed care, Mrs. Price. And I'll admit I'm disturbed to learn that he walked out without either of you seeing or hearing a thing."

She sniffed. "Well, I'm sure that detective who called will find him."

Oh, crap. That detective had probably called before Lindsay had made it down the driveway. He wanted to pin the murder on her or on poor Shane. Why work when you can go for the easy answer?

She knew what she had to do: find Shane before Detective Deperro did.

But first she had to figure out why Shane had taken off. Only one possibility leaped to mind. He could have gone out to the highway to hitch a ride to some bigger city where he imagined he could live on his own until he turned eighteen. When she thought about it, Randy was a big man who might have reminded Shane unpleasantly of his father and uncle. Lindsay had thought Shane understood that he'd be with the Prices for only two or three days until a suitable foster home was located, but even if he sort of trusted her, believing that the next placement would be any better might be beyond a boy like Shane.

It bothered her that he hadn't had any stuff of his own to take with him. Thanks to police planning to search his uncle's house, they couldn't get into it at least until tomorrow to collect the duffel with his belongings. He wouldn't have any money, either—unless he'd taken some out of Althea's purse. Lindsay wasn't about to ask and put any ideas in the woman's head.

"If you'll excuse me, I need to look for him," she said. "Obviously, I won't be bringing him back here."

Randy's jaws bulged. "We wouldn't have a boy who'd sneak out like that."

Walking down the sidewalk to her car, Lindsay rolled her eyes. Really? Every kid they'd taken in was a saint? She was angry enough; she intended to contact a colleague and suggest they reconsider the Prices' receiving home license.

She hadn't reached her car when an unmarked police SUV rolled up behind her bumper. Deperro got out and watched her approach. She felt a tiny bump in her chest, because there was no denying he was a magnificent male specimen—six foot two or three and broad-shouldered, with dark hair and eyes and bronze skin—but he'd done or said nothing to make her think she'd *like* him. So she nodded vaguely in his direction and went around to her driver door. She couldn't think of a thing she wanted to say to him.

His deep voice carried well. "Ms. Engle."

That tone would scare Shane, too. She really had to find the boy first. "Detective."

"Can we talk?"

Gee, he'd asked.

Only after she opened her car door did she face him. "We've already done that. You may research my background and job performance to your heart's content, but I think I'll get an attorney before I sit down with you again. Now, if you'll excuse me." Not looking at him again, she climbed in behind the wheel and gave a yank to the door handle, only to meet resistance.

Somehow, he'd moved fast enough to grab hold of the top of the door.

Lindsay turned a blistering glare on him. "What do you want?"

"You to tell me where I might find Shane."

"How can I? My best guess is that he decided he can't trust any adults. It would appear he's right."

Those espresso-dark eyes narrowed. "His uncle was murdered. You don't think it would be irresponsible of me *not* to sit him down for a talk? To think, oh, his caseworker says he's a *nice* boy. He couldn't have anything to do with this, and think how much I'd upset him by asking where the hell he was while someone was beating Uncle Martin's head in."

Lindsay tried very hard to hold on to her dislike, but that was hardly fair. Of course, his job demanded he find out where Shane had been while Martin was being killed. Ask Shane if he knew who might hate Martin—or benefit from his death.

Her keys were biting into her palm. Not looking at him, she said quietly, "I really don't know where he is. I'm…scared for him."

There was a moment of silence. He moved again, squatting inside the open door so he was closer to her eye level. Lindsay was painfully aware of the way the fabric of his black cargo pants stretched across powerful thigh muscles. She hated being torn between so many conflicting emotions and impulses.

"I understand," Deperro said, in an entirely different voice. "Believe it or not, I'm concerned about him, too."

She made herself meet his eyes. "Why?"

It was obvious the detective wasn't sure he wanted to tell her, but after a moment he rolled his shoulders as if to release tension. "What if the uncle saw him on the street and grabbed him? Shane might have had reason to fight back. Or what if he was there in the house when someone else killed his uncle? Did he run before that person had a chance to get a hand on him, too? Or did he see something he's afraid to tell anyone?"

Lindsay was afraid her mouth had dropped open. He was right. Those were real possibilities she hadn't considered. Shane might be in danger because he was only a kid standing with his thumb out beside a highway. But he might be dead, too, or running from a killer.

All the air in her lungs left her in a rush. "None of that occurred to me," she admitted.

"You could help me do my job."

If Shane were here, wouldn't she encourage him to answer Deperro's questions?

Of course she would. "For the third time, I really, truly, cross my heart, *don't* know where he is. I don't have the impression he has any good friends. How could he, when he didn't want anyone to know how bad it was at home?"

"Yeah," the detective said gruffly. "I get that."

"My best guess is that he's running away because he didn't like the Prices and is afraid of what will happen to him once he's placed again. He might think he can get by as a street kid in Portland or Seattle until he ages out."

Deperro swore. "I'll put the word out to watch for him. Damn. We want to stop him before he gets too far."

Again, he was right. And he was able to marshal

help from sheriff's deputies and even the state patrol in a way she couldn't. Had she really thought she'd find Shane by driving aimlessly up and down local roads?

Deperro frowned. "Could he have gone by his uncle's house to pick up his stuff?"

"Would he dare?"

"It's worth looking." He rose easily to his feet and stood gazing down at her.

"I can go out there while you—"

"Head out there, too." His eyebrows rose, giving him a devilish look. "You're welcome to join me."

Lindsay closed her eyes. As much as she hated to surrender, she just about had to.

"One question," he said.

She braced herself.

"Has Shane ever been caught setting fires? Even small ones?"

Remembering the smell of something burning at the Ramsey house, Lindsay was profoundly relieved to be able to shake her head. "No. Never."

The detective's eyes stayed narrow and intent, but finally he nodded.

That didn't mean he believed her.

DURING THE DRIVE, Daniel coaxed Lindsay—she'd stiffly given him permission to use her first name—into telling him what she knew about both Martin and Austin Ramsey.

Shane's mother had died when he was nine. When Shane came onto Lindsay's radar, he'd admitted that his dad hurt his mother, too. He thought Dad had killed her, but didn't know for sure.

Daniel gave her a startled glance. "Did you report his suspicion?"

"No. I made a note in his file, but he wasn't home when his mother died, and he said his father denied having anything to do with it."

"How did she die?"

"She was helping paint the exterior of the house. Supposedly, Austin heard her scream and raced around to find her on the ground. She'd been atop a tall ladder, painting the trim on the eaves."

"A fall." Daniel heard how expressionless that came out.

"Hard to prove anything."

"Unfortunately." The odds of a woman whose husband had been battering her dying in an accident struck him as about a hundred to one, but there really wasn't much he could do all these years later.

"I should have done more of a background check on the uncle," Lindsay admitted after a minute, not looking at him. "Martin's ex-wife didn't return my phone call then, and I depended too much on Shane's confidence in his uncle. While I was at the hospital this morning, I finally reached Martin's ex-wife, who has remarried and lives back east. He hadn't abused the kids, who were really young when the divorce happened, but he'd hit her a few times, she said. He hasn't demanded visitation, but she said there was no way she'd let their kids go for an unsupervised stay with him."

"Have you let her know he's dead yet?" Daniel asked. Fingerprints had already confirmed the victim's identity.

"No, I thought you might prefer to do that."

"I would." He was surprised at her restraint, although it was possible she just hadn't wanted to do a death notification. Who did? "You're sure she wasn't here in Oregon when you talked to her?"

"Pretty sure. I reached a cleaning lady at the house, who gave me Mrs. Schulze's work number."

"Took the new husband's name, huh?"

"Apparently."

He kept eyeing Lindsay sidelong, wondering if she'd just tamped down the hostility or whether she had let some of it go. Not all, or she'd be willing to look at him. And why would she, once she guessed he had to consider her as a possible suspect in the murder of the man who'd brutally beaten the boy under her charge?

Truthfully, Daniel couldn't see it. He'd walked out to the woods where she thought she'd seen someone watching her, but found nothing. Given the extremely dry ground, the guy would have had to do something as stupid as drop a cigarette butt to leave any evidence of his existence, and he hadn't. That's if he existed at all. But Daniel wouldn't hold it against her if she'd been scared enough to imagine someone.

Earlier Daniel had gotten the quickie summation of her job history. Apparently, she had received nothing but sterling reviews by supervisors in Child Protective Services. A few quotes from her annual reviews said things like, "Really cares for the kids," as well as "Lindsay is practical, kind and refuses to let down a child who counts on her." If the supervisor was to be believed, she was adept at dealing with the abusive adults as well as the children. She had a talent for matching adults and children with the right therapists, too.

She'd done social work for nine years, the last three with CPS. If she hadn't yet cracked and knocked off a vicious abuser, why would she now?

Of course, cops were known to break eventually, too, and do something they wouldn't have ten years before or even a month before. While Daniel couldn't entirely rule her out as a suspect, he was more interested in Shane, and then in gathering information from neighbors, friends and people who'd hired Martin along the way. If the man had been capable of losing it with his nephew the way he had, he could have lashed out at other people as well.

At Martin's house, Daniel parked, turned off the engine and looked at Lindsay. "I'm taking you in with me because you'll have a better idea what Shane had with him and whether anything is missing. I'll ask you not to touch anything and to stay with me."

She retorted, "Why are you treating this like a crime scene?"

"Because trouble could have started here and followed him to his brother's house."

Her clipped nod managed to convey surface agreement underlaid by skepticism.

Daniel had the keys that had been in Martin's

pocket. It took him a few tries to find the right one to open the front door. It led directly into the living room, which lacked any suggestion of a woman's influence. Scratched, worn hardwood floors were matched by dingy off-white walls, unadorned by art. Instead, a big recliner faced a flat-screen TV. The sofa seemed an afterthought.

His nose twitched at the trace of an unpleasant odor. Lindsay's eyes widened and her head turned. She locked her fingers together at her waist. "Is that…?"

"Something dead? I don't think so." That would be an all-too familiar odor for him. This wasn't the singed smell that had permeated the kitchen at the crime scene, either.

She didn't look all that reassured but followed him to the kitchen. He almost gagged when he pulled the trash from under the sink.

"Can we relax the 'don't touch' rule long enough to throw this out?" she asked, making an awful face.

"Once I poke through it." He'd found useful evidence in garbage cans or dumpsters before, but felt certain that wouldn't be the case here.

When he donned latex gloves, Lindsay retreated a few steps. "You're braver than I am."

He smiled. "I doubt that. Cowards don't do your job."

Those blue eyes flashed at him. "You're right about that."

Beneath dirty food containers and a bunch of beer cans, he found a pound of hamburger that was now gray and all too clearly the source of the stench. Daniel took the plastic bag out to a garbage can he'd noted during the earlier visit. Lindsay stayed on the back porch, sucking in fresh air.

"None of that looked recent," she said when he returned.

"No." He'd noticed the same.

"But…does that mean neither of them had dinner the night before last?"

"Let's look in the fridge."

"Do we have to?" she mumbled.

Daniel outright grinned as he swung open the refrigerator door. Another package of hamburger wasn't looking good. Otherwise, racks held mustard, mayonnaise and ketchup, a half gallon of milk—nearly empty, he discovered, when he lifted it—onion and celery in the vegetable drawer, and a pizza box on the top shelf. He took it out and decided it was still edible. He tipped the open box toward Lindsay.

"I suppose that was dinner."

"His, maybe. More would have been gone if Shane had had some. He's a teenage boy."

Her eyes glittered with anger he understood. "You're saying the creep beat him because, what, he didn't throw away some wadded paper towels and a few beer or pop cans?"

"Something like that," he agreed.

"I assumed Uncle Martin had cooked, with the understanding that Shane would do the clean-up." That anger still carrying her, she said, "Can we check out Shane's room?"

"You know which one it is?"

"I was with Shane when Martin helped carry his stuff up. Saying how glad he was to have Shane, and how he wished he'd known how his brother had treated his own son." She shook her head in disgust. "Apparently, the abuse was okay for him because Shane wasn't his."

They started up the stairs. To distract himself from the sway of her hips in front of him, Daniel commented, "In my experience, it's not usually the good guys who get murdered. It's drug dealers, gang members, people trying to screw other people over. The exception is victims of domestic abuse."

She waited for him on the landing, a crinkle forming on her forehead. "This is a turnaround for you, then."

"When this happens, it's usually because a woman or an older kid fights back. Grabs a knife or gun." He shrugged.

He almost regretted saying it, because wariness showed on her face again. "That's why Shane is at the top of your list."

"I'm afraid so," Daniel admitted. "I won't railroad him, Lindsay. I promise."

She searched his eyes with an intensity that shook him. He wasn't used to suspecting someone might have actually seen parts of his psyche he'd rather keep hidden. As a cop and a former soldier, he had plenty he never talked about. He didn't look away, though; he wasn't sure he could.

Finally, she dipped her head, indicating—what? Acceptance? Belief in him?

He could only hope.

One step into Shane's room and Daniel knew the boy had been here today and was gone. Dresser drawers remained open. Lindsay peered under the bed, urged him to open the closet door. Empty.

Finally, staring into the closet, she said, "At least he has his stuff."

If that was the good news, he didn't want to hear the bad.

His phone rang while he was locking the front door, Lindsay having already started down the porch steps. Unfamiliar number, but local area code. He answered.

"Detective Deperro, this is State Patrol Officer William Lasher. I have the boy I was told you're looking for."

"That's good news." He was aware of Lindsay stopping, turning to look at him. "Where did you find him?"

"The kid had gotten a surprising distance from Sadler. He'd had his thumb out on Highway 97 near Redmond."

"I'll come pick him up," Daniel said.

"Oh, we're on our way to you. Can't say the boy is happy—" there was a smile in Lasher's voice "—but he's gobbling a double cheeseburger and fries, so I'd say he's okay."

Daniel laughed. "Hey, he's a teenage boy. Bottomless pit."

"That's for sure. I have two of 'em at home."

Daniel thanked him and they agreed to meet at the Sadler police station. He could see from Lindsay's expression that she thought he'd isolate the kid in an interrogation room and take out his rubber hose.

"I want to sit in on your talk with him," she said firmly.

"You're entitled," he agreed. "Unless you or we come up with another family member willing to take responsibility for Shane, you'll need to stand in as his guardian."

She eyed him suspiciously, then climbed into his SUV. Lindsay Engle was one feisty woman, who wouldn't appreciate his smile.

THE BOY STARED anxiously at Daniel. Small for his age, he looked downright pathetic with the bruising in full color, the swelling that distorted his face, and the way he held one arm across his torso as if protecting it. Daniel had broken ribs before and knew how painful they were. Shane's right hand was wrapped to immobilize several fingers, which would rule out writing or texting. The still grossly swollen lips turned his speech into a mumble.

Lindsay had very gently hugged him and murmured something in his ear. Now she sat on the boy's side of the table, where she could fix a distrustful gaze on Daniel.

"Are you making me go back to that foster home?" Shane asked her.

Lindsay shook her head. "No, we've found a permanent placement for you. You'll like this family."

Not hard to see Shane's doubt.

"Why did you leave the Prices' home?" Daniel asked. "Ms. Engle has been worried about you."

Shane shot a quick look her way. "I'm sorry. I just thought…" He didn't finish.

"Did either of the Prices do or say anything that frightened you?" she asked him.

His shoulders hunched. "Not really. He—Mr. Price—looked mean."

Enough chitchat. "When did you last see your uncle Martin?" Daniel asked.

The kid's puzzlement appeared genuine. "Yesterday morning. When he said I had to go to school and to get out of the house."

"Has he contacted you?"

"How could he?" He sounded confused. "I don't have a phone or anything like that."

"He could have had his call put through to your hospital room."

"The only person who called was Ms. Engle." His expression changed. He drew into himself, appearing to shrink. "Is he trying to get me back? Like, claiming it wasn't *him* who hurt me?"

"No—" Lindsay broke off at Daniel's signal.

He said bluntly, "Your uncle is dead, Shane."

Shane gaped. "*What?* How?"

"He was murdered. Ms. Engle found his body."

His wild stare swung between Daniel and Lindsay.

"But… I don't get it." And then he drew in a sharp breath. "You think *I* killed him?"

Daniel modulated his tone. "I have to ask, Shane. The fact that you were missing at the same time he was murdered doesn't look good."

"I wouldn't! I never saw him!" He focused on Lindsay. "I didn't!"

She reached for his uninjured hand. "It's okay. Just answer Detective Deperro's questions so he can eliminate you as a suspect."

Well, at least she hadn't said, *I believe you,* although Daniel felt sure she did.

Trouble was, despite a usually cynical nature, he believed Shane, too.

Chapter Three

Shane eyed the molasses cookies Rhonda Manning had set out. She and her husband, Lyman, both beamed at him. Lyman designed games for a small software company in Bend. He worked remotely three days a week, only going into the office the other two days. Maybe five foot nine or ten, he was as scrawny as Shane, and certainly not physically prepossessing, which made him a good choice for Shane.

Lindsay thought this was the perfect home for Shane.

She smiled at Rhonda. "If you don't mind me snitching a cookie or two, I'd better get back to the office."

"Of course not. I'll grab a napkin."

Lindsay turned to Shane. "Remember your promise to the detective."

Shane ducked his head. "I won't run away again. If I freak, I'll call you."

She laughed, hugged him and murmured in his ear, "You do that." Lindsay thought he was smiling when she let him go, although given the swelling on his face it was a little hard to tell.

Shane was shyly reaching for a cookie when she thanked the Mannings and left.

Unfortunately, she'd lied; she wasn't going to the office. Her destination was once again the hospital. As medical personnel were legally required to do, an ER doctor had contacted Child Protective Services to report his belief that a twelve-year-old girl was being sexually abused by her stepfather. Lindsay's supervisor, Sadie Culver, had asked her to take this investigation. The only other caseworker free to pursue it was male, and Sadie assumed the girl would feel more comfortable with a woman. Given that Deperro had allowed Lindsay to take Shane, exacting only the promise that he stick around, she thought she had the boy settled. She couldn't forget that she had dozens of other open cases, but the most urgent leapfrogged to first place on her agenda.

Nobody in Kaila Kelley's family had appeared on the Oregon Department of Human Services' radar before. That wasn't unusual in cases of sexual molestation; those children rarely told anyone what was happening. Shame and threats were such an effective one-two punch that a father could work his way through three or four daughters before even a hint of the ugly situation surfaced. Lindsay hated knowing that Kaila had an older sister, Kira.

She learned at the hospital that the observant ER doc had admitted Kaila over the objections of her mother. Going to her room, Lindsay found Mrs. Norris sitting solicitously at her daughter's bedside. The slight figure in the bed lay curled on her side, looking toward the window instead of her mother.

When Lindsay introduced herself, Kaila rolled over, her small face with delicate bones drawn with anxiety. The mother jumped to her feet.

"I just don't understand why that doctor insisted on calling CPS!" Anxiety underlaid Mrs. Norris's anger. "My husband thinks of Kaila as his daughter. He'd never do anything so awful! She had to have been raped, maybe by a boy at school. It's the police who should be investigating."

They would be, but Lindsay didn't tell her that. Rather, she said calmly, "I'm here to find out what Kaila says happened."

Mrs. Norris turned her head to look at her daughter. "Tell her." Her voice rose to near-hysteria. "Tell her your daddy wouldn't hurt you."

Before the girl could open her mouth, assuming she intended to, Lindsay took two steps to place herself between the mother and child. "I know this is difficult for you, Mrs. Norris, but I need to speak to Kaila alone. You can wait in the hall or go down to the cafeteria and get a cup of coffee or lunch. If you give me your phone number, I can—"

"I have a right to be here! I'm her parent," the woman cried.

"Under usual circumstances, that's the case. However, we need to offer the children we protect the chance to speak freely to us. I feel sure you understand that."

Paige Norris understood no such thing, but eventually, reluctantly, withdrew.

"Hi, Kaila." She sat in the chair pulled close to the bed and smiled sympathetically. "I'll bet you have awful cramps."

Wary brown eyes focused and unblinking, Kaila nodded.

"Are your parents divorced? Do you have contact with your biological dad?" Lindsay already knew, but this seemed like a good way to edge into the difficult part.

"Daddy died," Kaila said in a small, husky voice. "In a car accident."

Lindsay touched the girl's nervous hand. "I'm sorry. It's hard to lose a parent."

Tears shimmered in Kaila's eyes but didn't fall.

"When did your mother remarry?" Lindsay asked.

"Four years ago. I was eight."

"That's been a long time. Do you think of your stepfather as your dad now?"

The girl shook her head vehemently. "He's mostly nice. You know? But he always liked to hug us and we had to sit on his lap and stuff like that. Mom said he's just touchy-feely. Like that. I didn't like it, but I just—" She broke off.

I just endured it. That's what she wasn't saying. And her mother had sent the message that she should ignore her own instincts and allow a man to handle her any way he wanted. Lindsay had to struggle for a moment with her temper.

Once she had it mastered, she asked, "What about your sister? Kira? Does she like him?"

"Uh-uh. She hates him. She never said anything, but I think he did *this* to her before. I'd find her crying, and she'd tell me to go away."

"And what is 'this'?"

Getting a child her age to spell out the details took patience. But Lindsay sat quietly and allowed Kaila to take her time. Finally she admitted to the molestation, but her eyes glistened with tears when she said, "He told me I couldn't tell *anyone*, or bad things would happen."

Starting to weep, she exclaimed, "But I can't go home! I can't!"

Lindsay took her hand and said firmly, "No, you won't be going home unless and until we're certain you'll be safe there. I'll call the police, and they and I both will talk to your mom, your sister and your stepfather. In the meantime, I'm placing both you and Kira in a foster home. She can't stay at home, either."

"Really?" Those wet eyes held a glimmer of hope. "Mom says I'm lying. That's what she'll tell you, too."

"You know what?" Lindsay smiled. "I've heard that before. What *you* tell me is what counts the most."

Kaila cried afresh, but less with despair than relief, Lindsay thought.

"Now, you'll be staying here at least overnight," she said. "I'm going to talk to your mother now. I'm also asking the nursing staff not to allow either your mother or stepfather in to see you. Okay?"

She gave a big nod and started swiping at her face with her sheet.

Lindsay squeezed Kaila's hand and turned her mind to foster placement options.

DANIEL TIPPED BACK his desk chair and brooded. Not surprisingly, he'd had little luck finding any of Martin or Austin Ramsey's neighbors at home midday. He'd have to canvass the neighborhood in the early evening. So far, he hadn't come up with names of friends, either. He supposed he'd have to start with clients who had hired Ramsey to work on their homes or businesses; the guy had kept records of his jobs and payments. Daniel wasn't optimistic about learning much from them. The brutality of the beating shouted rage. This crime was personal. It had to be.

Most murders weren't mysteries. Wife shot husband after he hit her one time too many. Brawls got out of hand at bars. A creep holding up a convenience store panicked and shot the clerk.

On the face of it, Shane was the likeliest—and best motivated—suspect, and Daniel couldn't yet 100 percent rule him out. The fire in the trash can was typical for the budding arsonist. Nonetheless, Daniel thought the kid was sad more than angry, and the timing wasn't right. After all, Daniel couldn't be sure the fire was connected to the death, although setting a can in the middle of the kitchen floor to, say, burn papers didn't strike him as logical.

Anyway, now that the medical examiner had established time of death, Daniel didn't see how the boy could have managed to knock off his uncle while also picking up his stuff from his former home and getting so far from Sadler. Suspicious by nature, however, Daniel reminded himself that Shane might have an older friend who helped by driving him around... and possibly even with murder.

He couldn't rule out Lindsay Engle, either, if only because he had to look twice at the person who'd found the body. He considered her unlikely, in part because, while CPS workers had a tough job and did burn out, what happened to Shane wasn't extreme or anything new to her. He hadn't read any undertones in what she'd said. In fact, he liked her determination to protect a boy who'd taken some hard knocks—literally and figuratively. He liked a lot more than that about her, but kept that kind of interest tamped down.

"Hey." Another Sadler detective, Melinda McIntosh, tapped her knuckles on his desk.

He straightened with a jerk. Damn, he should have noticed her approach. Way to go.

"What's up?"

"I just caught an investigation that involves a woman I hear you know. Lindsay Engle?"

Unexpectedly jolted, he said, "Tell me about it." Had he read the social worker wrong?

Melinda grimaced. "The lieutenant likes to give me anything that involves female victims."

"That's...sort of logical," Daniel pointed out.

"Yeah, but it's also sexist." She shook her head.

"Forget I said that. This involves a girl who was apparently raped. She's named her stepfather."

Daniel shook his head in disgust. He also relaxed, although he hoped not visibly. "And Ms. Engle was assigned to the case." He was proud of himself for not calling her Lindsay, for keeping his distance.

"You got it."

Midthirties, Melinda was divorced and attractive, with hazel eyes and dark hair kept in a severe bun. There was a time Daniel had considered asking her out, but her appeal hadn't overruled the likely complications. Instead, they'd become friends who worked together well when partnered on investigations. That was happening more since Daniel's previous partner had turned out to be corrupt, taking money to protect drug traffickers. Daniel never would have called John Risvold a friend, but he had trusted him. Being shot, twice, by his partner had been convincing evidence that the guy had betrayed not only Daniel, but everything else they were supposed to stand for.

"Ms. Engle is good at her job," he commented now. "Really good. Don't get between her and the kid she's protecting."

Melinda laughed. "You mean, if I don't want to lose a hand?"

He grinned. "Something like that."

Her smile faded. "With these kind of accusations, it isn't easy hanging on to any objectivity."

"No, it isn't." He hesitated. "Yell if you need backup."

She waved off his offer. "No reason I should."

Didn't that sound like famous last words? Unsettled, he watched her walk out of the cramped detective bull pen.

AT FIRST MEETING, Doug Norris seemed a likeable man. Lindsay saw what Kaila had meant. He was medium height, his body soft without being fat, his smile friendly. His handshake was soft, too, and possibly a little damp. Nerves?

Lindsay hadn't expected him to admit to having a sexual relationship with one or both daughters, and she'd been right. Instead of outrage, he went with deep disappointment. He loved the girls, had done his best to fill in as their father, couldn't understand what had set Kaila off.

"You are aware of the reason she was hospitalized."

"Don't some girls have heavy, er, cycles?"

Cycles? He couldn't possibly be that prudish, given that he was married and outnumbered in his home three to one by females.

Lindsay repeated the doctor's observations, with his conclusion: Kaila's bleeding had denoted an injury from an act of nonconsensual sex described as brutal.

"Brutal?" he repeated. *Now* he sounded outraged. "I can't believe that. Her mother said Kaila looks fine. She couldn't understand why that doctor wanted to keep her."

His reaction cemented Lindsay's certainty. He didn't think what he'd done was brutal; he'd probably convinced himself that his stepdaughter was happy to have greater intimacy with him. He wouldn't consider himself a violent man.

She asked further questions. Well, yes, he'd been home with Kaila when the alleged assault occurred, but all they'd done was watch TV. If it was true that she'd been hurt, she must have slipped out of the house later, met up with some friends. She was protecting one of them.

Kira insisted her stepfather had never done anything like that to *her*—until she found out that she was being removed from her home along with her sister no matter what she said. Then she cried and admitted he'd been molesting her for several years. She hated him, but Mom wouldn't listen and she didn't know what to do.

The phenomenon was all too familiar to Lindsay. Life was tough for a woman raising two children on her own, especially if she didn't have the skills to make an adequate living. Once she'd found a nice guy who treated her well, she didn't want to admit to his dark side. If she pretended even to herself that her daughter's accusations weren't true, that said daughter was acting out as she entered her teenage years, then everything was fine. Kira would be ashamed someday at the awful things she'd claimed. So would Kaila, who must have gotten the idea from her older sister.

Lindsay had also encountered plenty of women who leaped immediately to their children's defense and called the cops themselves. Unfortunately, Paige Norris wasn't of that breed.

By the end of the school day, the foster care coordinator she liked best to work with had found a foster home that could take both girls. Keeping them together was important.

She spoke several times to a Detective McIntosh. Honestly, Lindsay had been surprised that Sadler PD had any women on the force, never mind one promoted to detective. This was a traditional, conservative town, to put it mildly. Melinda McIntosh must be both tough and determined to have earned her place.

They'd agreed to interview family members separately, since their goals and authority differed. Detective McIntosh strongly supported Lindsay's decision to remove both girls from the home while the investigation progressed.

Late in the day, Lindsay checked on Shane, learning that he was in the middle of a computer game designed by his new foster dad, and was in awe at how impossible it was to beat.

She also spoke to Kira and Kaila's foster mother, who said they were settling in well. Kira came on the phone to say, "Mrs. Simpson is really nice, except she says I have to go to school tomorrow even if Kaila doesn't."

Laughing, Lindsay said, "Since Kaila spent last night in the hospital and you didn't, that sounds fair to me."

The silence that followed sharpened her attention. Finally, voice small, the fourteen-year-old said, "I wish I'd told, 'cuz then this wouldn't have happened to her."

"Kira, when the person you most rely on doesn't

believe you, you have to ask yourself why anyone else would. You also have to know that, if someone in authority actually *does* believe you, it'll mean your family getting torn apart. That's scary."

"How do you know? Did…did this happen to you, too?"

"I had an abusive parent—" not something she often admitted "—but it wasn't sexual."

"Oh." Kira was quiet for a moment. "I guess it hurts either way."

"It does."

The conversation stayed with her when she returned to the office to do some online research and write reports. For a girl at such a tumultuous age, Kira Kelley was astonishingly insightful and mature.

Lindsay felt confident that the two girls were telling the truth about their stepfather. His "poor me, I'm just trying to be a great dad" crap confirmed their stories. Mom's emotions and responses were off, too. Still, there wasn't any more Lindsay could do until results came back on the rape kit and Detective McIntosh tied up her investigation.

A thought slithered into her head. Too bad Doug Norris hadn't been murdered instead of Martin Ramsey. After this last beating, Shane would never have been sent back to stay with his uncle, but a judge might decide to return Kira and Kaila to their mother and stepfather if no proof was found to support their accusations.

Guilt rushed through Lindsay. How could she even *think* something like that? Yes, she despised men like

Doug Norris with every fiber of her being, but violent impulses were foreign to her. She had vowed long ago never to be anything like her mother.

Besides, it was unlikely Martin's abuse of his nephew had anything to do with his murder. He had to be involved in something shady, or he'd hurt someone who wanted revenge, or maybe he had been sleeping with a married woman. The timing would turn out to be coincidental. She refused to believe otherwise.

Chances were good Detective Deperro was pursuing other avenues of inquiry—wasn't that the right term?—and she wouldn't hear from him again.

And no, that wasn't a twinge of regret she felt. It was probably her stomach reminding her she hadn't stopped for lunch.

THE ONLY UNEXPECTED finding once the medical examiner opened up Martin Ramsey was several tumors in his lungs.

"Squamous cell carcinoma," the M.E. remarked. "Those tumors can extend into the wall of the chest."

The blackened lung gave away the dead man's lifetime of smoking. Daniel had seen the ashtrays in his house, smelled the tobacco smoke that had seeped into the walls.

"Didn't get a chance to kill him," he said.

The small fire set in the wastebasket hadn't had anything to do with Martin's smoking. No cigarettes had been found in his pockets, and Daniel hadn't smelled even a hint of tobacco smoke in Austin's house.

Dr. Stamey had already expressed his belief that the weapon used to bash in Ramsey's skull was an old pipe, perhaps two inches in diameter. He had plucked flakes of rust from the mess that was the victim's head.

In his first pass through Austin's house, Daniel hadn't seen anything like that, nor had the CSI crew.

Now that he knew what to look for, he intended to return to the house. He had yet to search the several outbuildings, although he didn't really expect to find the weapon. The killer had probably brought it with him, and taken it home when he or she was done. He or she would have worn gloves, too. His gut said this murder had been planned; it wasn't an impulsive act. The rage was there, but it might have been boiling for a long time.

What made Daniel uneasy was the fact that Martin had been beaten to death, as he had beaten Shane only the day before. Hard not to connect the dots. Coincidences didn't sit well with him.

He didn't make a habit of jumping to conclusions, though, or accepting easy answers like a fish snapping up the fly. He had work to do, and plenty of it.

An hour later, he was sitting in a conference room at the county jail questioning Austin Ramsey, who sat across the table from him. Austin was close to Daniel's height and breadth, as his brother had been. His hair was barely stubble and he had a cauliflower nose. Either he'd been in a lot of fights or he'd boxed in his younger years.

"Martin's dead?"

This was the third time Austin had said that, as if he kept hoping for a different answer. He was even shedding some tears, swiping angrily at them with the back of his hand. He could beat his own kid but cry over the death of his brother. Sentiment came in many guises.

"He is." Daniel hesitated, then told him about the cancer. "If you're a smoker, too, you might want to see a doctor."

"Nah, I never started up." He scowled. "You gonna find who killed my brother?"

"Yes, I am. I'm hoping you can help."

"Any way I can," Austin agreed.

As the big brother started spilling everything he knew about Martin, Daniel reflected that sometimes you had to dance with the devil, like it or not.

And then he wondered how Melinda's investigation was going…which brought him to thinking about Lindsay Engle. He gave his head a hard shake to get her out of it, causing Martin to pause midsentence and gaze at him in surprise.

"Sorry," Daniel said. "Just…had a passing thought. You were saying that he hadn't been seeing any woman steadily recently. Anything stand out about the women he did see?"

"He didn't say nothing about anyone. Maybe he was taking a rest."

A rest. That was one way to put it. Daniel had been taking a rest, too, no one catching his eye.

Until Lindsay Engle had, at a highly inconvenient time.

Chapter Four

"I know it's frustrating that the job was left unfinished," Daniel said drily.

Perched on the wingback chair facing him, Cathy Haugen showed her embarrassment with a flush. "I'm so sorry. Someone murdered him, and I'm complaining because he didn't show up here the next morning and finish spackling the wall around my new window."

He was interviewing the homeowner because Martin Ramsey had been working for her the week before he was killed. So far, Daniel hadn't learned much from her. As a detective, he wasted too much time talking to people who didn't turn out to know a thing. Sooner or later, he had to remind himself, something useful would pop.

Ms. Haugen agreed that she and Martin had chatted. He'd mentioned a nephew living with him, but she didn't recall the boy's name. No, Martin hadn't seemed any different the last few days he'd worked here. Well, the last day, maybe. He'd been quieter than usual.

After thinking, she said, "Brooding." And then he just hadn't showed up the next day.

Because he was dead. Daniel chose not to remind her of that cold, hard truth.

Time to wind this down, he decided. He'd opened his mouth to thank her when his phone rang.

"Excuse me," he said, rising to his feet and walking toward the patio doors before answering the call from Detective McIntosh. "Deperro."

"Daniel, I told you I'm investigating the sexual molestation of a girl, Kaila Kelley."

His interest sharpened. Kaila Kelley, whose caseworker happened to be Lindsay Engle.

"I had an interview scheduled with the stepfather," she said tersely. "I found him dead. Murdered. I thought you'd be interested."

"I am. Are you still at the scene?"

"CSI hasn't even arrived. I called you right away. There might be a connection with that murder you're already investigating."

Because of Lindsay's involvement, or did this guy's injuries resemble Ramsey's? Daniel didn't ask. He'd see soon enough.

"Address?"

After committing it to memory, he made his excuses to Ms. Haugen, gave her his card in case anything should occur to her and left.

Ten minutes later, he pulled to the curb behind the crime scene unit's van and a marked SPD car. The unmarked maroon sedan at the head of the line was

Melinda's. Curtains were probably twitching up and down the block.

At this house, blinds were drawn on the front window. The minute a uniformed officer opened the door and handed him a clipboard to sign in, Daniel smelled smoke. Through an archway, he saw the body and two crime scene investigators he knew in the living room. One was taking photos. Although Melinda wasn't in here, he detoured to take a look at the victim.

He winced at what he saw. Doug Norris had been stripped naked and posed. The handle of a knife stuck out from his chest. From the quantity of blood, Daniel guessed the blade had torn right through Norris's heart.

He had no trouble interpreting the message. Norris had been raped and his heart broken. Exactly what he'd done to his stepdaughter.

This fire had been set in a copper kettle on the hearth that probably held newspapers or kindling during the winter. Today, it had been stuffed with paper of some kind that had burned down to ashes. The fire had leaped up high enough to char the white-painted brick fireplace surround. Not intended to burn down the house, but then this killer had staged the body with care. He—or, damn it, she—wouldn't want that effort to go to waste.

One of the techs glanced up and greeted Daniel, who nodded in return. This was an ugly crime, but they would all do their jobs. Compartmentalize, which meant tucking away what they'd seen before they went home to their families.

He found Melinda in the kitchen on her phone. He waited until she ended the conversation and set down the phone.

"You saw?"

"I saw," he said. "This wasn't subtle."

"No. I gathered that Martin Ramsey was beaten, just like he'd beaten the kid. That could have been chance, but when I saw what was done to Norris…"

"We have two kids who were badly injured. Now the assailants are dead in a way that resembles what they did to the kids. I couldn't be sure about Ramsey, but after this—" Daniel shook his head. "I hope you don't mind working together. The small fires at each scene are as good as a signature. We have one killer."

She nodded. "I agree. But what is he trying to tell us with these fires?"

"I wish I knew," he said in frustration. "How old is the girl?" If she'd said, he didn't remember.

"Two girls," she corrected him. "Kaila and Kira. Twelve and fourteen. Turns out he's been raping Kira for a couple of years. Now, Kaila. I don't like to say a victim deserved what he had coming, but I'll make an exception for this creep." After a discernible pause, she added, "That's assuming, of course, that he really was guilty."

Daniel knew what she believed. "This killer didn't wait for you to gather enough evidence to be ready to file a charge. We have a sort of vigilante who has killed twice now, and only four days apart. That's fast for someone who has never before committed murder."

"Are we sure he hasn't?"

Turning so he could see a slice of the living room, Daniel grimaced. "I looked for anything similar in Oregon. Choice of victim, use of a fire as part of his MO, attack meant to mimic what was done to the victim. Unless our killer's a recent transplant—"

"And then how did he learn about the assaults on these particular children?" Deeper than usual lines etched her face. "No, you're probably right. We just have to figure out what triggered this guy to start now. The assault on Shane Ramsey sounds as if it was savage, but not that unusual."

He knew what she meant. There was a reason Child Protective Services had a unit here in Sadler the size they did. Child abuse was all too prevalent, pretty much everywhere.

He didn't like saying this, but had to. "Is it coincidence that Lindsay Engle is the caseworker involved in both instances?"

Melinda frowned. "She's been with the unit for several years. Besides, she's been good to work with. I don't want to believe she's capable of anything like this."

"I don't want to think she is, either," Daniel said roughly. "But I can't help noticing that, except for the wastebasket fires, she's all that ties these two murders together." He frowned. "She know about this yet?" He nodded toward the living room.

Melinda shook her head. "I haven't even notified the wife. I suppose we'd better confirm the whereabouts of the two girls, although I can't imagine…"

He couldn't, either. Doug Norris had been average size rather than big and brawny, but he'd still have been a lot stronger than any young girl—even two of them trying to take him on at once. Just thrusting the knife in so deep required more strength than most people realized, as well as some knowledge of how to direct the blade under the rib cage and upward to reach the heart. As a method to kill, it wasn't for the squeamish. And then there was the suggestive staging. By two kids with no history of trouble or gang affiliation? No.

A woman who had spent years building rage toward this kind of offender? Who'd had plenty of time to do her research, who although slim had appeared fit, whom Norris would have let in the front door?

Like it or not, Daniel and Melinda had to seriously consider Lindsay as a suspect.

LINDSAY WAS LESS than thrilled to pick up the phone to hear the receptionist say in a hushed voice, "There are two detectives here to see you."

Wonderful. Was Detective Deperro still fixated on her, or did he have more questions about Shane?

"Send them back," she said, then wished she'd asked for their names. This could be different detectives, here to see her about another case—except the SPD didn't have a very big investigative unit.

She rose to her feet and braced herself. Maybe she wouldn't feel any impact from Daniel Deperro's presence this time.

Wrong. Even though he allowed Detective Mc-

Intosh to precede him into the room, she saw only him. Daunting shoulders, dark eyes, unreadable expression. She had the sense that he saw only her, too. She couldn't be imagining that.

The other caseworkers present lifted their heads from whatever they were doing to watch the pair of detectives weave their way through desks to Lindsay's. Silence fell over the room.

Detective McIntosh nodded civilly, although she, too, had an air of reserve Lindsay hadn't felt when they talked yesterday.

Deperro said coolly, "Ms. Engle."

So much for being on a first-name basis.

"I can grab another chair." Lindsay looked around.

"Do you have a conference room available?" the woman detective asked. "It would be better if we had some privacy."

A chill spreading inside her, Lindsay said, "Of course." They followed her to a room designed for small groups. She took a seat and waited, from long practice keeping a pleasant expression on her face. Once they, too, had taken seats around the table, she asked, "What can I do for you?"

Detective McIntosh jumped in. "Well, first I wondered if you'd had a chance to talk to Doug Norris again."

Surprised, Lindsay focused on her. "No, I haven't even tried. As I told you, until you've completed at least an initial investigation, I won't make any further contact with either the girls' mother or stepfather."

"That's what I understood," she said.

Deperro didn't bother with the niceties. Without any trace of the warmth she'd glimpsed in him when he persuaded her to work with him to find Shane, he said, "Can you tell us what you have done and who you've seen this morning?"

The chill deepened to the point where Lindsay wondered if her core temperature had dropped.

"I had to put a bunch of investigations on the back burner for Shane and then Kaila and Kira. I've managed today to talk to half a dozen people regarding allegations made by neighbors, teachers, in one case a school nurse."

"Did you speak to them here?" Deperro asked brusquely.

"No. I made appointments to meet them at a coffee house or at their homes. In one case, at a school." She looked from one face to another. "I've worked with officers from SPD often and been cooperative, but I'm getting a bad feeling here. This meeting is over unless you tell me what happened to bring you here this morning with your current attitude."

They didn't even exchange a glance, and yet she could feel communication humming between them.

It was Detective McIntosh who inclined her head. Big surprise there; she made a far more natural "good cop" than would her partner.

"I had an appointment this morning to speak to Mr. Norris. When I arrived at the Norris home, I found him dead." She paused. "Murdered."

Lindsay quit breathing, only stared. Dizzy, she

sucked in air at the same time as she pushed her chair back from the table. "And you think *I*—"

In his deep voice that now sounded like a growl, Deperro said, "I'm sure you'll agree that we should be concerned by the fact that you're the caseworker for both children whose guardians were murdered within forty-eight hours of you removing the kids from their custody."

She couldn't look away from his hard, accusatory face. It was absurd to feel hurt, even if they'd worked together and she'd caught him watching her in a way that surely meant he was attracted to her. Maybe all he'd been doing was softening her up. Face it, he'd made no bones about his suspicion after Shane's uncle was killed.

Doing her best to shake off the hurt, Lindsay rose to her feet. "I won't meet with either of you again until I have an attorney present. You know your way out. Please excuse me."

"Ms. Engle."

Her back to him, she stopped in the doorway.

"If you'll just give us your schedule for the morning, let us verify that you didn't have a gap of time—"

She kept walking.

"SHE *HAS* BEEN COOPERATIVE," Melinda said mildly. "Did you have to come on so strong?"

He'd been a jackass, Daniel knew that, without quite being sure why. He'd been…relieved earlier on to be able mostly to dismiss her as a suspect in Martin Ramsey's murder. He liked her. He could more than like her, which had to be the problem. Now, after the second murder, he was infuriated to suspect she'd played him, manipulated him from the get-go. Maybe he was mad most of all because she exerted a pull on him that was damn near irresistible. Now he felt betrayed—and that was dumb as hell. In his heart, he couldn't believe she was a killer. To eliminate her, he had to ask questions—but if he'd come at those questions differently, he wouldn't have alienated the woman who was, at the least, a central witness in their investigation.

A woman who was unlikely to lower her guard around him again.

Melinda had every right to come down a lot harder on him than she had so far.

He scraped a hand over his jaw. "I'm usually smoother than that."

Perturbed lines showed on her forehead. "Yes, you are."

"Maybe if I leave, she'd talk to you."

Her eyebrows lifted. She didn't have to say, *Fat chance.*

Lindsay was nowhere to be seen as he and Melinda passed back through what resembled a squad room, the half dozen occupants unashamedly staring. Had he thought she would return to her desk and continue calmly doing her job? She was probably closeted with her supervisor…or out shopping for a criminal defense attorney.

He called himself a few names, but he kept his mouth tight and his face blank. Out front, they passed the reception desk, Melinda nodding politely to the woman who was on the phone but also keeping a sharp eye on them.

He pushed open one of the double glass doors to let Melinda go first.

Behind him, the receptionist called, "Wait!"

He turned to see she had hung up the phone. "Yes?"

"Ms. Engle left something for you."

A mousetrap, to break a few of his fingers? He doubted she could come up with a cherry bomb that fast.

The receptionist handed over a manila folder, so thin it couldn't hold more than two or three sheets of paper. He didn't open it until he was in the car. Behind the wheel, Melinda leaned toward him so she could see, too.

Two pages. The first was a copy of today's page from a day planner showing that, indeed, Lindsay had jam-packed her morning with appointments. Page two, scrawled names and phone numbers.

Though angry, she'd still given them what they had asked for.

"If she actually met with all these people, I don't see how she could have worked in a detour to kill Doug Norris." Tone still mild, Melinda was going out of her way not to sound critical.

Squeezing a murder into this schedule looked pretty damn unlikely, Daniel had to concede. His mood lightened a little—but they still had to verify that neither Lindsay nor another party had canceled one of these meetings.

"Do we know TOD?" he asked.

"Jim Stamey texted me. Said his best guess for time of death was three to four hours ago, but may change his opinion after the autopsy."

Daniel nodded. Stamey would have checked the body's temperature and half a dozen other indicators before venturing his opinion. In Daniel's experience, the guy had never been far off.

"That puts Norris's death at somewhere between nine and eleven this morning," he calculated.

"Yes. I suggest we notify the wife and find out when she left for work. That might narrow the window."

"I'll make some calls from this list while we're on our way." That would also serve the purpose of distracting him. He hated being a passenger.

Without further comment, Melinda backed the department-issue car out, swung around and made the turn onto the street that led to the light at the highway. He didn't know where Paige Norris worked, but obviously Melinda did.

By the time they pulled up at an insurance office downtown, Daniel had spoken to three of the people Lindsay had met with that morning. So far, so good…but he had yet to reach three more people, one of whom hadn't answered or responded to the message he'd left.

Inside the insurance office, he had his first look at Paige Norris, who didn't yet know she was a widow.

From behind a desk she lifted her head to beam at them before she really saw them.

If not for Ramsey's murder, he'd be looking hard at this woman. With the abuser now out of the picture, she might get her daughters back. What if she really *hadn't* believed the girls' claims, but her husband had given himself away and now she knew they'd told the truth? Women were known to do the unthinkable to protect their children.

This woman, though…she was petite and appeared ultra-feminine, wearing a fuzzy pink cardigan over a matching pink top. His gaze fell to her long fingernails, also painted pink. It would be hard to kill a man without breaking a nail or chipping the polish.

Unless she'd managed a quick visit to a manicurist on her way to work. Could those be fake nails?

Sometimes he wished he didn't so readily suspect people of the worst behavior.

In this case…he couldn't imagine she'd beaten a large man to death as a cover for when she murdered her own husband.

Alarmed, Paige Norris shot to her feet. "Why are you here?" She was all but whispering. "My bosses don't know anything about the girls and…and all the ridiculous stuff they said. I could lose my job if—"

"We need to speak to you." Melinda could sound tough when she needed to. "Is there a conference room available?"

"I—" Mrs. Norris drew several deep breaths as if to steady herself. "Yes. I suppose." She hustled them halfway down a short hall and into a plush room with a table surrounded by six upholstered chairs. "I'll be right back."

Daniel heard her talking to someone a short distance away, explaining that she needed to speak to someone about an issue at school and could this someone else please answer the phone for a few minutes.

Apparently the coworker agreed, because she reappeared, whisking into the conference room and yanking down a shade over the inset window before taking a seat and gazing at them anxiously. "Now what?"

Daniel deliberately chose a chair off to one side. Melinda was familiar to the woman; she'd respond better to her questions. Observing felt like the smarter tactic.

Too bad he hadn't kept his damn mouth shut earlier with Lindsay.

"First, let me ask what time you left home this morning," Melinda said.

Her anxiety increased. "I don't understand." It took some low-key urging, but finally Mrs. Norris said, "Eight forty-five. I usually leave at eight-thirty, but Doug was unsettled about having to talk to you, and—" She stopped. "Wasn't he home? I know he intended to be."

"Mrs. Norris—Paige—I'm afraid I have some bad news for you."

She pressed a hand to her throat. "What could possibly—"

"When I arrived at your house, the front door was unlatched and open a few inches. I called for your husband, and when I didn't receive a reply, I stepped inside. I found him dead, Mrs. Norris. He was murdered."

The woman let out a piercing cry, the kind that haunted cops who made too many death notifications.

MAD AS HELL but also a little scared, Lindsay explained to her supervisor what was going on.

Her boss for a year now, Sadie Culver had been brought in from the Bend office when Glenn Wilson retired. She'd been thrilled with the promotion and especially the transfer, because she and her husband, a third-generation cattle rancher, already lived near Sadler. Lindsay guessed her to be in her early forties, and both liked her and had found her to be a supportive manager.

Sadie was aghast to learn that the police might suspect one of her caseworkers of a crime as horrific as murder.

"You're the last person I could imagine going off the deep end like that," she exclaimed. "I mean, with this job, burnout is always an issue, but you haven't exhibited any sign at all."

Lindsay sat facing Sadie's desk, feeling like a school child called in by the principal. "Thank you for saying that," she said, relaxing a little. "I understood why after the first murder the detective had to look at me, because I found the body. Now it's come down to me being the caseworker involved with both families."

"We don't have that big an office. If someone is

knocking off abusive parents, it could be chance that you were investigating both."

Lindsay shuddered. "What if someone really *is*? These two murders weren't even a week apart."

Sadie studied her with obvious concern. "Good Lord. I'll look to be sure our records haven't been hacked. Otherwise, how do you want to handle this?"

"I did give them my schedule for this morning. Unfortunately—" she hesitated "—that won't let me off the hook, unless Doug Norris was killed way earlier this morning. The problem is, I ended up with a break at about ten-thirty, when a mother I was to meet with wasn't home."

Her supervisor got an odd expression on her face. "You don't think there's any chance that woman, too, is…?"

It took Lindsay longer than it should have to understand. Sadie wondered whether the woman she'd had the appointment to meet with had been murdered. "Oh, dear God." She closed her eyes. "No, I can't imagine. Her son has had some bruises, but nothing that awful. I'm thinking the family might need counseling…but maybe I should ask the detectives to do a, um, welfare check on the woman."

"Have you tried calling her?"

"I did at the time and got voice mail, but I'll call her again right now." Her hands were actually trembling when she took out her phone.

A woman answered immediately. "Oh, is this Ms. Engle? I'm so, so sorry I didn't call to let you know I had to rush into work."

Jennifer James was a hairdresser.

"Mrs. James, I don't think you understand the gravity of the concerns that led to Child Protective Services being called in. You do realize we're authorized to remove children from their home if we believe them to be in danger."

Across the desk from her, Sadie let out a whoosh of air. Lindsay shared her relief, although her annoyance almost drowned it out.

Mrs. James expressed anger at the tattletale school nurse but also agreed to meet with Lindsay the next day.

Lindsay ended the call. "Well, she's alive."

Sadie leaned forward. "What can I do to help?"

"I can't think of anything at the moment, except to express faith in my mental health if either of the detectives shows up to talk to you." She made a face. "I think I need to take an hour of personal time right now, though, to find myself an attorney."

"Of course." Sadie stood and came around the desk, reaching out a hand to squeeze Lindsay's. "I can just imagine what Glenn would have to say about this."

Lindsay knew exactly what Glenn would say. Loudly. Probably to the police chief. "Let's not tell him yet, okay?" she suggested.

Sadie mimed zipping her mouth.

Lindsay produced something like a smile and headed back to her desk. She'd wait until she was in her car to do a search for attorneys and make her calls. Her fellow caseworkers did *not* need to know she was a suspect in a murder investigation.

Once she reached her car, she had to start it and turn on the air-conditioning to combat the August heat.

Maybe, she thought, as she flipped pages until she found "Attorneys—Criminal Law," whatever lawyer took her on would advise her not to speak to either detective at all. The burning in her chest told her how glad she'd be never to set eyes on Daniel Deperro again.

Chapter Five

When Lieutenant Matson walked out of his office the following morning, his gaze locked on Daniel. It didn't waver as he stalked across the bull pen, ignoring support staff and the only other detective present.

Uh-oh.

Daniel leaned back in his chair and waited.

The lieutenant came to a stop in front of Daniel's desk and crossed his arms. "Seriously? You've named a CPS worker as a suspect in two murders?"

Did he sound plaintive or annoyed? Daniel couldn't quite decide.

"We—" He cleared his throat. He had to leave Melinda out of this one. "I didn't go that far. All I did was ask Ms. Engle for her whereabouts around the time of the murder."

Middle-aged, Matson was softening around the waist but still formidable. "And do you have any real connection between her and these murders?"

"She's the caseworker involved with both families. Plus, these murders are to all appearances expressing rage at the abusers. In neither instance do the children have any family defending them, far less expressing anger. I questioned Ms. Engle after Martin Ramsey's murder but didn't take her seriously as a suspect. After the second murder…how can I not? Who else has reason to feel that kind of hate for two men who likely didn't even know each other?"

"Her supervisor is not happy. She feels we're endangering any future of interagency cooperation."

That was a load of crap, and Lieutenant Matson had to know it. Nonetheless, Daniel said, "You can assure her we're doing our best to eliminate Ms. Engle as a suspect as quickly as possible."

"Are we succeeding?"

"Unfortunately, she had a break in her schedule that would fit into the current estimate of time of death. I just reached the woman Ms. Engle was to have met with. This Mrs.—" he glanced down at his notes "—James says she had to rush into work and didn't think to let Ms. Engle know she wouldn't be home."

"Ms. Engle couldn't have counted on having any time."

"That does argue against her being the perp. Still, if she planned to go after Norris later, she could have decided to seize the chance."

Matson scowled, said, "Keep me informed," and walked away.

Everyone around them managed to look really busy.

THE ATTORNEY LINDSAY had decided on, Jeff Eimen, did indeed instruct her to refuse to meet with either detective without him sitting in. She had thanked him and paid a retainer.

Because she was a murder suspect.

You never knew what kind of new life experience might come along.

She decided to work from home for the rest of the day, making follow-up calls and reviewing files. Why not? That's what she did several evenings a week anyway.

Sometimes she felt as if she was drowning, but if she slowed down, a child somewhere would suffer. It was reality that abused or neglected children occasionally fell through the cracks. A caseworker left the job, another one replaced her but was somehow never given that particular file. Or a caseworker got involved in something messy and time-consuming, as with the Kelley girls, and assumed lower priorities could wait. She could be fooled by a seemingly sincere parent, misread a situation. The possibilities for disaster were endless, and ever-present. What if Shane hadn't survived the beating his uncle gave him, for example? How would she have lived with that?

Lindsay made herself push back from the desk in her home office and go to the kitchen to pour a cup of coffee and think about what she could make for dinner. That part didn't take long; a microwaveable meal it was.

She used to enjoy cooking. That was just one of many small pleasures and hobbies that had gone by the wayside over the past few years. She couldn't help wishing sometimes that she hadn't jumped onto the hamster wheel that was CPS, except she was always aware how urgently the job needed to be done.

Sighing, she took the fresh cup of coffee back to her desk. Her phone rang as she was sitting down. Since she recognized the number, she didn't answer. To hell with Detective Daniel Deperro.

The second time he called, she was on the phone with the grandfather of a child living with a drug addict mother. Deperro hadn't left a message the first time. She waited to see if he would this time.

Nope.

Five minutes later, her phone rang again and his number came up. Gritting her teeth, Lindsay answered coolly, "Detective."

"You've been ignoring me."

"Astonishingly enough, I haven't been sitting here playing computer games and waiting for you to call. I'm busy, Detective."

"I need to talk to you again," he said brusquely.

Annoyed to have his deep voice awaken a small thrill inside her, Lindsay said as distantly as possible, "I'll have to look at my schedule and coordinate with my attorney to find a possible time."

The ensuing pool of silence gratified her.

"Who'd you hire?"

"Jeff Eimen of Eimen and Sloan."

"Huh."

"You thought I was bluffing?"

"I hoped," he admitted. "You're making this more complicated than it has to be. For obvious reasons, I need to clear you. I'm not hounding you for the fun of it."

"Really? You could have fooled me." She let out a huff of air. This was pointless. "What I think, Detective, is that you tend to jump to quick conclusions. I'm right in front of you, so it's got to be me." She paused. "Now, if you want to suggest some times that would work for you, I'll call Mr. Eimen and run them by him."

"You were...good enough to cooperate today and provide us with your schedule. I need some clarification, that's all."

Even as she weakened, she knew she'd be a fool to believe that.

"I suppose you want to know what I did with the hour I should have spent with Jennifer James."

"That's one question," he agreed.

She closed her eyes and kneaded the painfully tight muscles in her neck. "I bought a chilled latte and a scone—orange-cranberry, if that matters—at the drive-through coffee place two blocks from the library. I then went to the city park by the Boys & Girls Club. I found a bench in the shade and ate my scone. To my current regret, I didn't see a soul."

"Did you receive or make any phone calls during that hour?"

"That's two questions, Detective Deperro. This is your last. I ignored several calls that weren't urgent, and I didn't call anyone. I enjoyed a slight breeze and meditated." The pain pinging up her neck hadn't relented. "Good bye, Detective."

"Wait!"

She ended the connection with her right thumb, then sat tensely waiting for him to call again.

He didn't. Not that he was done with her, of course.

"DAMN WOMAN," DANIEL GROWLED.

"I can guess who you're talking about."

Startled, he looked up. Once again he hadn't noticed Melinda's approach. Lindsay Engle was distracting, and more.

Jump to quick conclusions. That really had him stewing.

He told his partner how Lindsay claimed to have filled the hour she'd unexpectedly been given.

"We can check with the coffee kiosk," Melinda said thoughtfully. "Maybe find out who was patrolling that part of town this morning. He might have noticed her car, especially if it was the only one in the parking lot."

"Yeah. We can do that."

She perched on the edge of his desk, one foot braced on the floor, the other dangling. "What's wrong?"

"Has it occurred to you that she might be a target of the killer? Either he's trying to get her in trouble...or he thinks he's doing her a favor and she'll be thrilled."

Melinda frowned at him. "That's a leap considering she's a link between only two murders."

The chair squeaked as he leaned back, raising his eyebrows. "Only?"

She frowned. "You know what I mean."

"I do, and you're right. Her name coming up in both investigations really could be coincidental. I looked over the past few months to see what child abuse cases CPS has needed to involve us or the sheriff's department in."

"And?"

"Five, and three of them weren't anywhere near as horrific as the beating Shane Ramsey took or the sexual molestation of the Kelley girls."

He'd felt some relief at learning that. The odds were eight to one that the next really nasty case would be handled by a different caseworker. Nine to one if the supervisor directly handled investigations as well as managed the caseworkers.

He twitched at having to acknowledge how much he didn't want Lindsay to be a part of this.

"You expect more murders," Melinda said.

"I don't think this killer will stop. Do you?"

She pressed her lips together but finally said, "No."

"Unless we catch him."

"Does the lieutenant know what you think?"

"He hasn't asked, but he's not stupid."

They looked at each other for a minute. Finally, she said, "I've only been involved in a couple of murder investigations. One was a stabbing during a tavern brawl and the other a domestic. Not exactly mysteries. I'm not sure what to do next," she admitted, with a frankness that surprised him. Melinda hadn't made it to detective in the face of bias by displaying any uncertainty.

Daniel knew she'd just given him her version of a compliment.

"We need to continue investigating the people around each victim. One of the two killings could have been committed as a way to muddy the waters."

If he wasn't mistaken, Melinda tried to hide a shudder.

"That's kind of drastic."

"It is, but it's happened."

"You're saying the fires were just a trick," she said.

"A not-so subtle way to convince us we have a single killer who has an agenda that's related to the abuse allegations."

"When really one of the two victims was murdered for an entirely different reason."

"It's conceivable."

Melinda hesitated. "Do you really believe that?"

He told her the truth. "No. Especially given the question of how this killer knew about both abuse allegations and so quickly. My gut says we need to quietly look at the other CPS caseworkers, indignant supervisor included."

"Burnout," she said slowly.

"And maybe someone who doesn't like Lindsay Engle."

"Or likes her a lot."

He wasn't happy with either scenario.

LINDSAY DIDN'T HEAR a peep from the detectives over the following several days. Rather than reassuring her, the quiet made her more nervous. It felt like the eye of a hurricane.

She decided, for once, to take the weekend off. Truthfully, she'd rather not be assigned any more investigations for the time being. If something awful came in, Sadie could give it to someone else. Just in case the abuser was murdered, that would ensure the cops knew she didn't have anything to do with the killings.

Still…it was strange that she was the caseworker in both instances.

The first question to ask was why Sadie had chosen her to talk to Kaila Kelley, when she was still tied up with Shane's case.

Because I'm a woman, she reminded herself, but she knew that wasn't all. Since Glenn's retirement, their office had only three male caseworkers, five female, six counting Sadie.

Two of the female caseworkers were newbies. The others… In her heart of hearts, Lindsay knew she was the best. The most perceptive, the most patient, most skilled at dealing with all parties, from the endangered child to the abuser and any other family members. She was also one of the most experienced.

Hey, growing up in a succession of foster homes had taught her plenty.

If Sadie did prefer her, well, it wasn't like getting gold stickers on her paperwork or being trusted to run errands to the principal's office. No, it meant her getting assigned to the most shocking cases.

She knew what she had to do now: refuse any new

assignments. Sadie would understand her reasoning. Lindsay had plenty to keep her occupied for a few weeks, at least. And think how wonderful it would be to catch up. That wouldn't last, of course, but just once, she'd like to come home at the end of a workday and be able to take the evening off without guilt. Or even put in for vacation! The last one had been three whole days so she could attend her college roommate's wedding two years ago.

So she'd enjoy this weekend, even if it was already Saturday morning. Go somewhere overnight. Drive to the coast, maybe? After enduring two months of central Oregon's usual summer heat, it would be bliss to walk on a rocky beach in the fog and mist. More blissful if she had someone to walk *with*, but she couldn't get greedy. After all, her last date had been with...

She couldn't even remember his name. A firefighter, who'd had to cut their evening short for a callout. A forest fire, not a home fire, she remembered. A lightning strike had ignited it, and people had been evacuated from rural north county. Every local fire department had fought that one. He'd promised to call her when life was back to normal, but never had. She'd only vaguely noticed, because it turned out they had nothing in common except some sexual sizzle that burned out, on her part, after listening to him brag about his hunting prowess for forty-five minutes.

Come to think of it, the long drive to the coast didn't sound all that appealing. So maybe she'd go up to Mt. Hood. There were a lot of bed-and-breakfasts in the area, she knew. Surely she could find a vacancy.

Decided, she started throwing a couple of changes of clothes into a small suitcase. She'd added toiletries and pulled the suitcase to the small entry when her doorbell rang. She hesitated, between one blink of the eye and the next seeing Martin's body lying on the kitchen floor.

For heaven's sake, it was midday and there must be neighbors out gardening, kids riding bikes. The spurt of fear was an overreaction.

A fist rapped hard on the door.

Really?

She swung it open to find Daniel Deperro on her doorstep.

DANIEL ANTICIPATED LINDSAY'S REACTION. If she'd let him speak, he'd explain. But she didn't.

Eyes narrowing, she snapped, "Since my attorney didn't happen to drop by for breakfast this morning, you need to leave." She tried to shut the front door in Daniel's face.

He was too quick, inserting a booted foot. "Damn it, will you give me a minute?"

"I'll report you to your captain. This is harassment." She glared at him. "Or are you prepared to arrest me?"

The heightened color in her cheeks made her even more beautiful. Appealing. Unfortunately, anger was responsible for the warmth tinting her cheekbones, not arousal or shyness.

He kept his foot between the jamb and the door. "I'm not. I...actually have good news for you."

No relenting was visible.

"Uh...can I come in?"

Her expression was about as friendly as a jagged chunk of lava.

Suddenly appalled, Daniel wondered why he was really here. He could have called. *Should* have called, not shown up on the doorstep.

"Okay," he said, pulling back his foot. As he'd hoped, she didn't slam the door. "We verified your purchase at the Java Stop." They'd been able to do that right away. "An hour ago, I was finally able to talk to Officer Capek. Do you know him?"

Terse nod.

"He saw your car at the city park. Passed it three times during the forty-five minutes you told us you were there."

Her eyebrows challenged him. "Maybe I sneaked out the back side of the park and called a cab."

"An old lady lives right across the street from the Norrises. She'd have seen the cab." Unless Lindsay had had it drop her a street away. But Daniel didn't believe that for a minute. What killer would dare take a cab to a murder scene? Ask the cabbie to wait for him? What if he returned covered with blood?

Daniel knew Lindsay was smarter than that.

Her grip on the door eased. "*Somebody* was in the house, so why didn't she see them?"

Good question. If Mrs. Knudson had caught even a glimpse of the killer, he and Melinda would have had other leads to follow and not gone straight to the state Department of Health Services offices.

"Back slider was unlocked."

"But he still took a chance that someone would see him—what? Jumping the fence?"

"He did, but if he was watching and, say, saw two adults leaving for work from the same house, he could be pretty safe in thinking he wouldn't be seen."

"If only people paid more attention…"

Catching the dark tone, mixed bitterness and sadness, Daniel nodded. "Both of our jobs would be easier."

"How can people not see long-term abuse?" Lindsay's expression softened to bewilderment that he understood.

"Hard to figure," he said quietly.

She'd let the door fall open far enough for him to notice the suitcase behind her.

His eyebrows climbed. "Going somewhere?"

"Going…?" Her head turned to follow his gaze. "Oh, yes. I'm fleeing from the law, obviously."

His grin clearly startled her. "Took your time about it."

Lindsay scrunched up her nose. "I haven't gotten away even overnight in months." One shoulder lifted. "Seemed like a good weekend."

Keeping his voice soft, Daniel said, "May I come in?"

"I was just leaving… Oh, fine." She stood back.

The front door of the small rambler opened into the living room. Gleaming hardwood floors weren't usual for the era of the house. He bet somebody, maybe Lindsay, had added them at a later date. A huge braided rug in muted shades of rust and peach centered the sofa, an easy chair and two antique rocking chairs. The brick fireplace would be great in winter. He guessed the TV was in the antique armoire, the door of which was firmly shut. Two built-in floor-to-ceiling bookcases to each side of the fireplace took pride of place.

"Nice house," he said.

"Thank you." Now she did look shy. "Will you be here long enough for a cup of coffee?"

"I'd love one."

Instead of sitting, he followed her to the kitchen. Bright red tiles formed the backsplash beneath old-fashioned white cabinets. A red enamel teakettle and red-and-white-checked curtains accented the tiles and made this room, too, homey.

She had her back to him while she started the coffee, giving him a chance to admire her curvy body in tight-fitting jeans and a thin red T-shirt that hugged her generous breasts.

She definitely pushed his buttons, and not only physically. Daniel just wished she wasn't mixed up in this mess somehow. While she couldn't see him, he let his mouth twist. Okay, by being such an ass to her he might have squelched any possibility of taking this attraction somewhere even when this was over.

Assuming she shared it.

After standing on tiptoe to take two mugs from a cupboard and setting them on the counter, Lindsay faced him, her expression turned wary. "It occurs to me I surrendered too quickly. You still have questions, don't you?"

He could tell she knew the answer before he opened his mouth.

Chapter Six

"I do," he admitted, but held up a hand before she could shove him out the door and slam it in his face. "But they're the kind of questions I'm asking because you know the people concerned."

"You mean, the families?"

Her wariness would have deep roots, in part because keeping information about cases confidential was her default. And then there was his hot-and-cold behavior. Why would she trust him?

"If necessary, but I'm thinking more of people working in your field." He hesitated. "Your coworkers."

"What?"

She hadn't put quite enough force into that. Lindsay had to have some of the same ideas he and Melinda had.

Daniel rolled his shoulders. "Can we go for a walk? Or—" No, she'd never agree. But, damn, he felt restless.

She glanced toward her suitcase. "I really wanted

to get away." She sounded wistful. "Do something fun."

"Do you ride?" he asked.

"You mean, horses?"

He smiled. "Of course, horses. I'm not a big fan of motorcycles, not after scraping so many bodies off the pavement as a patrol officer. I live on some acreage outside of town, where I can keep my horses."

"More than one?"

"Five," he said. "Quarter horses. I breed my three mares. Only one of them has a foal by her side right now, though. A two-year-old is about ready to start under a saddle. I'm letting him put on some size to be sure he's up to my weight."

He'd swear that was wonder he saw on her face. He hadn't screwed up after all. She might not like him, but she was obviously horse-crazy.

"If you mean that, I'd love to go for a ride. Heck, by the time I got up to Mt. Hood, I probably wouldn't be able to find a place to stay anyway."

"In August? Maybe a cheap motel."

Lindsay made a face at him. "Give me a minute to change clothes."

While she raced upstairs, he studied the books on her shelves and speculated as to why she didn't have any family photos on her fireplace mantel or walls. They might be on display elsewhere in the house or tucked in a photo album she often perused, but somehow he doubted it. Her own history might explain why she'd committed to her line of work.

That got him to thinking about social workers in

general. Or, more specifically, Child Protective Services caseworkers. How many were motivated to do such a difficult job by backgrounds as abused children? That would surely make them more likely to burn out in a big way—and to feel the kind of rage this killer so obviously did.

Something to ask Lindsay, except he didn't want her to think he was digging into *her* background.

"Sorry to be so slow." She took the steps at a clip that had him instinctively moving to the foot of the staircase to catch her if she took a header. "My boots weren't where they're supposed to be."

Not cowboy boots, but brown leather ones clearly made for riding. Right now, he wore the flexible tactical boots that were most practical on the job. Once home, he'd change into worn cowboy boots.

She grabbed her purse and car keys. "Should I follow you?"

"No, I can bring you home later. Maybe we can stop for lunch." If he hadn't gotten her back up again by then.

Once on their way, she surprised him by expressing curiosity about his background.

"I grew up in this part of the state," he told her. "Near Prineville. My father was a second-generation citizen. My mother came to the US from Guatemala as a teenager with her parents, who were migrant workers. Dad has a cattle ranch, which wasn't for me. I have an older brother who will likely take over when Dad retires, if he's ever willing to." He smiled. "Mama will no doubt put her foot down at some point. Cooking for half a dozen ranch hands for years and years must get old."

Lindsay chuckled. "I would have said I like to cook, but not that much."

"What about you?"

"Oh, I grew up in Portland. Ended up here only because I was offered a job in Sadler right out of grad school."

"Family still there?"

Out of the corner of his eye, he saw her hands flex, as if she wanted to tighten them into fists but had stopped herself.

"No," she said finally. "Never knew my father. My mother drifted in and out of my life until the court finally terminated her parental rights when I was ten. I learned later that she died just a few years after that."

"Drugs?"

"Alcohol."

Daniel took a hand off the wheel and laid it over hers on her thigh. He gave her hand a gentle squeeze and then made himself let her go. He wasn't much for touching and rarely did on impulse, but her tone had bothered him. She'd sounded so damned composed, as if she were talking about a casual acquaintance's troubled childhood, not her own.

"I suppose I'm a cliché," she said after a minute. "Trying to fix other families because I couldn't fix my own."

He thought about that. "Given that you work for CPS, isn't it more that you're trying to rescue abused children because nobody rescued you?"

The glance she flicked at him was both startled and shy. "People did occasionally try to rescue me. Thus the foster homes. Actually, I learned to ride at one."

He really wanted to reach for her hand again. Just touch her. Again. But this was too soon, even assuming he ever decided to act on his attraction to her.

Uh-huh. When was the last time he'd taken a woman out to his place for a ride?

He had to struggle to remember, which meant he'd kept any women he'd been involved with at a distance.

Lindsay and he were both quiet for the last five minutes of the drive.

LINDSAY LEANED FORWARD after he turned onto the packed earth of a long driveway. "Is that your home?"

"Yes. I converted an old barn." His satisfaction showed on his face as he looked at the structure.

Lindsay felt a sudden pang of jealousy. She liked what she'd done to her house, but this… The exterior appeared to have been stained and a protective coat undoubtedly applied, but the lines of the old barn remained, up to the peaked roof that would shed snow. The hayloft appeared to be a balcony now. Huge windows and skylights no doubt opened up the interior, both the main floor and what looked like a loft.

"It's spectacular," she said, unsure if it would be appropriate to ask for a tour.

Smiling faintly, he parked by the converted barn rather than the long, low one that was presumably a stable and said, "Come on in and take a look if you're interested. I need to change my boots."

The interior was rustic enough that she guessed he'd used reclaimed wood for the few walls and the floor, which was glossy but not planed to the completely smooth surface she was accustomed to. Kitchen, dining and living areas flowed in a way that felt natural. Cabinets had been crafted of a knotty pine and the counters were brown granite streaked with gold. Daniel disappeared up an open staircase to the loft, and she ventured to explore the back of the main floor, where a few rooms were walled off by rough, aged lumber that might have come from the original stalls. She found a full bathroom, a home office and what was probably a guest room.

Lindsay sighed with pleasure. This wasn't anything she'd have expected from him. Especially when he was being a jerk.

When he came back downstairs, she asked if he'd done the work himself.

"A lot of it," he said, his head turning as if he assessed the quality of that work. "My brother helped, as did a couple of friends. I did a hell of a lot of research before I started. The idea isn't original, you know."

"I do, but it isn't common, either. This really is gorgeous, Detective."

His smile became crooked. "Can we go back to first names?"

Stung by a sharp memory of how she'd felt when he went on the attack, she said, "Maybe that's not smart," and with her head held high, went out the front door.

Daniel—Detective Deperro, she reminded herself—grabbed a black Stetson from a hook by the door, set it on his head and followed her. He didn't comment as he led the way to the stable.

He saddled two horses, both easily identifiable as quarter horses from their powerful hindquarters, one a blood bay, the other near black. The bay was for her. Giving Lindsay a boost up, he said, "Nessa is good-natured. Not a slug, but she'll read your mind whatever your skill level."

His gelding was Max, although both horses had lengthy names under which they were registered. The two-year-old, which he pointed out grazing in a nearby pasture, was Nessa's son.

They set out at a walk, broke into a trot and then a lope. Lindsay gradually let her body relax and flow with the horse's rhythmic gait. The sun shone, not yet as hot as it would be by midday, and the sharp scent of ponderosa pine and juniper was one of the world's finest perfumes as far as Lindsay was concerned. She felt happy, in a carefree way she rarely did. Beside her, Daniel rode as if he'd spent half his life on horseback—which he probably had, growing up on a ranch.

The land was gradually rising, the pines growing taller and closer together. Daniel drew his gelding back to a walk, and Nessa did the same without waiting for permission from her rider.

Lindsay stiffened, knowing that Daniel slowed to

a pace that would allow for conversation. Still, she turned to look at him. "Thank you. I don't get to ride often enough. If I had a horse—"

His mouth quirked. "You'd ride every day?"

"Do you?"

"When I get home before dark."

The weight of her job settled back on her shoulders. "I...don't have much time for recreation."

"I'm sorry this can't be just for fun." He sounded as if he meant it, but his dark eyes were, as always, hard to read.

Lindsay only nodded. "What is it you think I can tell you?"

"It's probably occurred to you that one of your co-workers might have gone off the deep end."

She pressed her lips together and stared straight ahead, not really seeing the landscape before her. It seemed wildly improbable that one of the men or women she worked with could have committed such grotesque crimes, but...*somebody* had. She couldn't help thinking she sounded like the shocked neighbors after a serial killer was arrested.

But he kept his lawn neatly mowed, and there was that time when my garbage can got knocked over and he picked it all up without asking for thanks.

Even so, Lindsay argued, "It's hard to imagine. We're a small enough office that I know everybody pretty well. Two are relative newcomers, but they're both young and idealistic."

"You must have started that way."

She still didn't want to look at him. Talking about

herself always made her feel uncomfortably vulnerable. She tended to avoid it whenever possible.

"Not in the same way. Growing up the way I did doesn't leave you with many illusions."

"No." He sounded thoughtful. "I don't suppose most people last long at CPS."

"There are some who make it a career. My former supervisor, for example. Sadie—the current supervisor—has been with CPS for almost ten years now. If I had to guess, it's the idealists who burn out the quickest. Their expectations are unrealistic. I see a lot of what I do as achieving small victories. Sometimes I change lives, but not often. Some of the calls we get are for suspicions of abuse that are true, but not as severe. If the parent or parents will agree to counseling, there's a chance to change the family dynamics before we have to take more drastic action."

"So your instinct isn't always to want to yank the kids from the home."

"If there's any hope, I prefer not to. The foster care system is less than ideal, you know."

"I've read about the problems."

"At some point, I might like to go back to licensing and supervising foster homes. It's another kind of intervention, and really important." Lindsay gave her head a shake. "I've been rambling. This doesn't have anything to do with what you asked."

"Not true," Daniel denied. "The more I know, the better I can judge whether a particular social worker is covering up serious rage."

She had to ask. "I want to think it's chance that

I'm the caseworker for the two families involved in the murders."

He was quiet longer than she liked. Somehow, the sharply defined angles of his face gave an impression of grimness. Lindsay wondered if he knew that the half roll of his shoulders was something of a tell. Stress didn't go to his stomach; it rode his shoulders and neck.

He glanced at her, his gaze somehow sharp. "I'd like to think so, too."

Speaking of stomachs, hers knotted.

"Somebody could be trying to please you," Daniel said slowly, "or get you in trouble."

She'd prefer option C, if it existed. Hoping he didn't see her shudder, she said, "Those are both horrible possibilities. I've already decided that when the next call comes in where the kid is hospitalized, I'm asking Sadie to assign it to someone else."

He tipped the brim of his hat. "Good idea."

Then, of course, he queried her about her coworkers. She felt as if she was betraying them by talking about them to a police detective behind their backs. She wouldn't have done so at all if she hadn't understood his reasoning so well. She dreaded going back to work Monday, when she'd have to look around and wonder. Was dark humor a healthy outlet, or a hint at hidden anger? Was outward serenity nothing but a cover? She'd evaluate expressions, feel uneasy whenever she caught a coworker's eye.

Would she dare get together with any of them on an evening or weekend?

As it was, she didn't share everything she knew. A couple of people had told her in confidence about their own backgrounds, in each case as bad or worse than hers. Those stories she didn't even consider sharing.

Finally, in frustration, she exclaimed, "I just can't believe any of them would do something like this."

Ignoring her outburst, he asked, "Have any of the men asked you out? Expressed interest? Watched you in a way that feels sexual?"

She knew he was hinting at his earlier option B. Somebody had given her a couple of very twisted gifts, but—

Please, no.

She blew out a breath. "Ray Hammond flirts with me, but he flirts with some of the other women, too."

"He hasn't asked you out?"

"Just for coffee. That kind of thing. I've…taken to making excuses."

She'd swear his jaw muscles had tightened.

"Anyone else?"

"Matt Grudin was already in the office when I joined CPS." As if that made any difference. "He really wanted me to go out with him. He was pushier than I liked." She turned her head to meet Daniel's narrowed eyes. "And don't you dare tell him I said that. He got the message. I think he's seeing another woman now. Anyway, I have to keep working with him."

She wasn't about to tell Daniel that she still caught Matt checking her out. Some women would have been flattered, but she didn't like it. She never encouraged him and tended to avoid crossing his path if she could help it. Unfortunately, his desk was just across the aisle from hers.

This time, the repeat of "Anyone else?" came out as a growl.

"No." The only other man in their unit, Emmett Harper, was at least five years younger than her, easy mannered and enthusiastic.

"What about the women?"

She explained that she liked some of the women she worked with better than others, but that was normal.

He asked a few more questions, but then let the subject go with an "Okay." His legs tightened, and the black gelding went straight to a lope.

Once again, Nessa followed suit. The mare knew who the boss was here, and it wasn't the stranger on her back. Nonetheless, the faster pace exhilarated Lindsay, especially as they gained speed to a gallop.

Despite everything, she felt herself grinning, maybe even laughing, and when Daniel glanced over his shoulder, she saw the flash of white teeth. For this moment, they felt connected.

When she slid off Nessa by the open doors into the stable, she said, "That's the most fun I've ever had being interrogated."

Daniel's laugh kicked off an arrhythmia in her heartbeat.

HE KNEW WHERE to start now: with Mr. Pushy, Matt Grudin, and Ray Hammond, who might or might not have gotten the "no" message from Lindsay. Once

Daniel had taken her home, he would run background checks on the two men.

And, yeah, he was letting this get personal. Some stalkers never openly expressed interest in a woman; she was just supposed to suddenly see him and exclaim her wild attraction to him. Her continued indifference was a crime in that man's eyes.

Daniel wasn't ruling out the women, either. Most if not all in the office were smaller and weaker than the two male victims—especially Martin Ramsey—but they had an advantage. Men tended to discount women. Not hesitate to let them in the door, turn their backs when they wouldn't on a male stranger.

Which got Daniel speculating. How *had* Norris been overpowered? Had there been a tap on the head that wouldn't be noted until the autopsy?

Right now, Daniel wasn't in any hurry to get back to work. Lindsay had unsaddled Nessa without any prompting, cross-tied her and was now brushing her. He smiled at the sight of the mare, head low, twitching her skin here and there to make sure especially itchy places got appropriate attention, lips drooping.

Now, if Lindsay had put her hand on *him*, he'd probably do the same.

"She's about to fall asleep on you," he said.

Lindsay's unshadowed smile felt like a kick to his chest. "I noticed," she murmured. "She loves this. Max looks annoyed instead."

"He has sensitive skin and is maybe a little lacking in patience." Hoof pick in hand, Daniel bent to lift a foreleg to check for small stones or any kind of debris that could irritate the frog. He was pleased to see Lindsay doing the same, then sliding a hand over Nessa's hindquarters before beginning to comb her luxuriant tale.

"Do you show any of them?" she asked.

"Max and I enter cutting horse competitions. Otherwise, no. I bought one of my other mares from a college student who didn't have time for her anymore. Apparently, they rated well barrel racing."

"That looks fun." Lindsay sounded wistful before she went to the mare's head and gently rubbed her poll and ran her fingers through the black forelock. Nessa responded by butting her head against Lindsay's shoulder, then nibbling at her braid. Lindsay laughed. "Sorry, I'm not edible."

Daniel had a contrary opinion on that, but he could hardly say so.

After they turned the horses loose in a pasture, Max trotted off and bucked just for the fun of it, while Nessa ambled to a spot of shade beneath an old oak tree and settled down, hip shot, for an apparent nap.

Lindsay was still smiling as she turned away. "Maybe I'll do that when I get home, too."

And maybe strip to no more than panties and a tank top, given the heat of the day. Daniel stayed a couple of feet behind to be sure she didn't notice how interested he was in the idea of her sprawled on her sheets.

The buzz at his hip was the distraction he needed, even if he didn't want it. He opened the driver side door of his truck and glanced at the screen of his phone.

Dispatch. Never good news.

Lindsay had opened her door, too, and pulled herself up onto the seat, but she was watching him.

Even as he answered, he held her gaze. "Deppero."

"Detective, we just had a call from the sheriff's department. They have a body, and they're wondering if it might be connected to the two murders here in town."

He'd actually intended to call the new sheriff, a rancher he knew named Boyd Chaney, to discuss the two murders. Gossip must have done that for him.

Chaney co-owned a ranch with a friend, who a year ago had helped hide a little girl who witnessed her father's murder. Once her whereabouts were discovered, all hell erupted. At the memory, Daniel felt an unhappy twinge from his thigh. That was the day when he'd been shot in a gun battle worthy of the Old West.

Chaney had been so pissed off at the lack of help from the sheriff's department, that fall he'd mounted an election challenge and unseated the slug who'd held the office for twenty-four years.

Shaking off the thought, Daniel asked, "Address?"

When the dispatcher told him, he said, stunned, "There's a murder victim *at the sheriff's ranch*?"

Lindsay's vivid blue eyes widened.

"If I understood him correctly," the dispatcher said primly.

"They have a name for the dead guy?"

He couldn't look away from Lindsay, who he'd swear hadn't blinked in at least a minute.

"Yes," the dispatcher said, "he's apparently an employee. Howie Haycroft. That's all I know." Next thing he knew, she was gone.

"Damn," he said softly, swinging in behind the wheel. He stowed his phone between the seats and slammed his door.

"Did you get a name?" Lindsay asked, her apprehension not well hidden.

In the act of inserting the key, he went still. "Can I count on you not repeating what I tell you to anyone at all?"

"I swear."

He wouldn't have told her at all if he hadn't wanted to find out if she knew the victim. Specifically, whether she'd ever investigated him for child abuse.

And, man, he wanted her to look puzzled and shake her head.

"Howie Haycroft."

Her forehead creased as she thought. "Howie…? No, I don't remember…" Horror crossed her face. "Haycroft. Howard Haycroft. Oh, dear God."

He could echo that. "Your case?"

"Yes, but… Oh, it has to have been three years. It was one of my early ones."

"Crap." Daniel could have said something a lot stronger. "Whoever this is has access to the CPS files."

Her teeth chattered before she squared her shoulders, pulled on her seat belt and lifted her chin. Composure restored—on the outside.

"Will you tell me what you remember?" he asked.

"I can tell you the basics. You'd find it in court records anyway."

"Let's have it," he said grimly, and fired up the engine to take her home.

Chapter Seven

Daniel parked in front of the sprawling log ranch house that was County Sheriff Boyd Chaney's home. The second partner of the ranch, Gabe Decker, had had Daniel out to his own place for barbecues and the like a few times. Daniel would call Decker a friend, but despite several meetings he didn't know Chaney as well.

Chaney must have heard Daniel's truck coming, because he waited on the deep porch that ran the length of the house. A big, fit man, he came close to Daniel in height.

Climbing the porch steps, Daniel said, "Chaney." He let a crooked smile form. "Or should I say Sheriff?"

The man grimaced. "Make it Boyd."

"Where's the body?" Why waste time on small talk?

"Bodies." Boyd's eyes met his. "We found a second one."

What the hell?

"I'll ride with you," Boyd said. "Worker housing is half a mile or so north, beyond the barns."

Daniel didn't say anything until they were on their way. By then, he'd decided where to start. "What makes you think these killings have anything to do with the ones I'm investigating?"

"Now that I have access to law enforcement databases, I found background I didn't uncover when I hired Haycroft and his son Colin 'bout two years ago. Neither of them had ever been convicted of a crime, a red flag I look for. Boy was only eighteen then, but a hard worker. Increasingly lousy attitude, though. He didn't like being told what to do, especially by women. Resented our foreman, too."

"Leon Cabrera?" Like Boyd and Gabe, Leon was an ex-army ranger and had been or should have been a sniper.

Boyd's face set in hard lines. "I was about to let him go."

Was? Strong hint that Howard Haycroft's son was the other victim, not a surprise after Lindsay's description of the mess the Haycroft case had been.

"How about Haycroft?" he asked.

"Smart enough to keep his mouth shut, but kids learn from their parents."

Ahead, what had to be twenty log cabins had been built scattered about among a few acres of tall ponderosa pines. Each would feel private, not institutional like most company housing. Native plants formed an understory beneath the trees. The soil itself was tan

and gritty, bright green lawns and flower beds con-
spicuously absent.

Boyd nodded ahead. "Last cabin on the end."

Turning in, Daniel parked again, but neither man
moved to get out.

"Colin was almost seventeen when he spoke out
for his father," Daniel remarked. The background
Lindsay gave him explained why the son had been
condemned to share his father's fate. Despite the evidence to the contrary, Colin had insisted the father
wasn't abusive.

"It was three against one." Anger glinted in Boyd's
eyes. "Why did investigators believe the one kid?"

"I haven't taken the time to dig into the police investigation yet. I was a detective at the time, but I
didn't work that one. I'll pull out records once I'm
back at the office. When you called, though, I was
with the Child Protective Services caseworker who
did her own investigation after the death."

The word *death* being a euphemism in this case.
Howard Haycroft's wife had been executed. Hands
duct-taped behind her back, ankles duct-taped, too.
There'd been a single, fatal shot to the head from behind. Classic.

Expression arrested, Boyd said, "This the same
caseworker in both of the recent investigations?"

"Yes. We had to look at her, but we're ninety-five
percent sure she's no killer. That said, we've passed
the point where we can pretend it might be coincidence that she was the caseworker involved with all
three families."

Boyd grunted his agreement. He opened his door, but before getting out, said, "I think you can guess how they were killed."

Yes, that wouldn't be a surprise.

LINDSAY COULDN'T SETTLE down after Daniel dropped her at home. Not Daniel, she reminded herself; she'd be a fool to drop her guard yet. Detective Deperro.

Since it was lunchtime, she heated a can of soup but ended up dumping most of it down the drain before rinsing the bowl and putting it in the dishwasher. She couldn't concentrate on the mystery she'd been reading. Daytime TV held zero interest for her. Every sound from outside had her skin prickling for no reason she could name.

All she could think about was Howard Haycroft and the destruction of his family.

He'd killed his wife. Lindsay would swear he had. The scene had been carefully constructed to look like a home invasion, from what she'd heard. Thank God she hadn't seen that body.

The police determined the back door had been jimmied *after* Marcia Haycroft was killed, not before. She had either let the murderer in or he'd already been in the house. Lived there.

Police suspicions explained Lindsay's involvement. She temporarily removed all four kids from the home, although the oldest boy refused to stay in the receiving home, and she had eventually given up and let him go back to his father.

The three younger children, two girls and a boy,

cried abuse. Their bodies showed evidence of enough healed broken bones, scars and burns to back up their claim. The oldest son, though, whose name she couldn't recall, had insisted furiously that the mother had been the abuser, not his dad. The others were making up stories, he'd insisted.

She got the feeling the younger children were afraid of their brother as well as their father.

In the end, the DA declined to file charges of murder against Howard, claiming a lack of forensic evidence. No witness stepped forward. That left the fate of the children in the hands of family court. Howard wanted them home, but in the end the judge ruled that the three youngest children would go into a foster home, having supervised visits with their father until they regained confidence in him.

Her stomach had lurched at the idea of the children pressured into agreeing to go back to him, but the visits didn't go well and finally petered out.

Last she'd heard, Howard and his almost adult son sold the house and moved away. Idaho, she thought. She hadn't heard anything about the Haycrofts in a couple of years. Now she wondered if Howard had resumed contact with his younger children. Tomorrow, she'd contact the foster care supervisor with DHS.

But unless something had changed drastically—if one of the younger Haycroft children had been killed or committed suicide, for example—why punish Howard now? And who would care enough to bother? There'd been no adult relatives willing to take in the children, far less avenge them.

And, dear God, what did *she* have to do with it? Lindsay would rather think that somebody hated her than that these murders were supposed to please her.

It almost had to be one or the other, didn't it?

She paced, going from window to window, not seeing what was in front of her eyes. Instead, she grappled with an ominous sense of losing control. She felt horribly as if she were stuck in a web, waiting for the spider.

MELINDA MADE IT out to the ranch while the crime scenes were still being processed. Daniel had forgotten she, too, had met Boyd Chaney at least once, in her case when she'd come out to the ranch to question three-year-old Chloe Keif about how much she'd seen when her entire family had been wiped out. Despite a necessary, tough veneer, Melinda was good with children. He was puzzled by the tension he read between her and Boyd, but made sure neither would guess he'd noticed it.

Both men accompanied her when she studied the two scenes. With the CSI crew borrowed from the state still working, neither body had been moved. Howard's was in the cabin, requisite trash can with the ash of burned papers beside him, while Colin's body was in a storage shed. The fire there had been set on the dirt floor, a safe distance from anything else flammable. Seemed the killer hadn't wanted to start a forest fire.

Melinda waited until they reached their vehicles

to ask, "Could he have been involved in his mother's murder?"

"Lindsay says he appeared to be shocked and grieving her loss. No indication from the younger kids that he had anything but a good relationship with her."

"So you're suggesting this boy was brutally murdered just because he defended his father?"

Boyd said, "More because he single-handedly saved his father from being charged with murder or child abuse. *And* labeled his brother and sisters as liars."

She seared him with a glare. "You know he was probably scared, too."

"I didn't find him very likeable," Boyd commented with a mildness belied by the razor intensity of the stare that answered hers.

"So it's okay he got killed?"

"I didn't say that."

Time to intervene. Daniel pushed himself away from the fender. "Can we focus?"

Melinda took a deep breath, then another. Looking toward the cabin, she said, "I guess the first thing we have to ask ourselves is who is taking primary on this one."

Boyd's eyebrows climbed. "It's my jurisdiction."

The two of them were going to start another pissing match? Daniel barely refrained from rolling his eyes. Instead, he shook his head and offered a solution.

"We cooperate. We bring Sheriff Chaney up to

date with our investigations so he doesn't have to
start from scratch. We don't keep anything from each
other."

Boyd smiled slightly.

Melinda's lips thinned, but she kept her mouth
shut.

"Do you plan to assign a detective to this?" Daniel
asked Boyd. "Or work it yourself?"

"I'll assign my senior detective, but look over his
shoulder. He has zero experience with a murder investigation, but he might as well learn."

"Unless you were military police," Melinda put
in, "you don't, either."

"I've killed people. Seen friends go down. Does
that count?"

Daniel was starting to get a headache. Clearly, he
needed to take point where the sheriff's department
was concerned.

"We don't have many murders in the county, not
counting domestics or bar brawls. We all learn as we
go." He was the one exception, having worked major
crimes including homicide in Portland for a couple of
years before deciding to come home to eastern Oregon, but he didn't say so. Melinda probably knew,
and the last thing they needed was this to become a
three-way tug-of-war.

"Fair enough," Boyd said. "I'd like to join you
to interview the caseworker, even if you've already
talked to her. I'll have my detective canvass my other
employees to find out if they heard anything or saw
anyone around the Haycrofts' cabin. Or, for that mat-

ter, anyone unfamiliar out here on the ranch. If you can email me whatever you have so far, I'll let you know what I learn from the CSI team."

"Good. Let me give you my phone number."

Melinda offered hers up, too. Daniel couldn't help noticing that Boyd didn't enter it in his phone. Because he had no intention of talking to her? Or was it already in his contacts because they had some sort of previous relationship?

None of my business.

MONDAY MORNING, LINDSAY parked as close to the front door of the office as she could manage. If only the back door wasn't kept locked.

Two journalists with microphones in hand and cameramen to back them hovered by the double glass doors. Did they know what she looked like, or could she slip in with a head shake and "no comment"?

The latest murders had been the lead story on local news and featured in eastern Oregon newspapers as well as the *Portland Oregonian*. Unfortunately, journalists had been able to access public records and find her name.

She grabbed her briefcase, closed her eyes and took a few deep breaths, then jumped out. Her car beeped behind her as she used her key fob even as she hurried toward the entrance.

"Excuse me!" one of the men called. "Are you Lindsay Engle?"

The second journalist, a woman, stepped between

her and the door. "How do you explain your involvement with the families preceding all four murders?"

"I have no comment for you. Please let me by."

"Have the investigating officers interviewed you?" the man demanded to know. "Do you have the sense you're considered a suspect?"

Shaking inside but outwardly composed, Lindsay met the woman's eyes. "If you don't step out of my way, you'll be speaking to the police yourself."

The reporter moved, her expression huffy. "We're giving you an opportunity to share your perspective."

Hand on the door, Lindsay paused. "You should respect the fact that Child Protective Services keeps names and the results of investigations confidential. Speak to the police detectives."

She slipped inside, the closing door cutting off their voices.

Dear God. How could she keep coming to work? But how could she not? This was what she did. Hiding out would make her look guilty. No, it wasn't an option.

Celeste Klassen, the receptionist, hurried around her desk, her wary gaze darting to the view through the glass. "Lindsay! You're okay?"

"Hasn't been the best week," she admitted. No, nearly two weeks now.

Celeste hugged her. "We've all been worried about you. What's happening is weird. And creepy."

Lindsay smiled wryly. "I totally concur."

"Sadie asked to see you as soon as you came in."

There was a surprise.

"Thanks." Lindsay went to her supervisor's office and found the door standing open.

Sadie glanced up from some paperwork on her desk. "Oh, Lindsay. Come on in. Take a seat." She set aside her reading glasses. "I'm sorry you had to run the gauntlet outside."

"Everyone else must have, too. Can't we ban them from the property?"

"That's easier when it's private property. State property is theoretically owned by all taxpayers."

Lindsay wrinkled her nose. "We still shouldn't have to be harassed coming to work."

"Did they recognize you?"

"They asked questions as though they did."

"Tell me about the Haycrofts. I wasn't assigned here then. I've read about it, but that's not the same."

Lindsay repeated what she'd told Daniel, and added a few details she'd withheld from him.

Her supervisor listened, interjecting only a few questions. At the end, she shook her head. "I'd say why now, but it was obviously one of our agency's more dramatic cases."

"And now it's even more so."

"Yes. What's most disturbing is that this murderer either has to be an insider or has somehow got access to our records. The IT department has looked but found no indication a hacker gained entry," she added. "That said, we both know there are people out there who can sneak past any safeguards."

Lindsay nodded her agreement.

Sadie picked up her glasses and began fiddling

with them. "For now, if I have to assign any new investigations to you, I'll keep them routine." She held up a hand, although Lindsay hadn't protested. "This is no criticism of you. I hope you know that. But... let's not tempt fate."

The ban, if that wasn't too harsh a word, might not be meant as criticism, but it didn't feel good, either. Call it a pointed finger, because she might not be at fault but was, in some roundabout way, responsible.

Since Lindsay had already made the same decision—but not yet discussed it with Sadie, she nodded and rose to her feet. "I'm going to try not to step out the door today. I'll have lunch delivered."

Sadie laughed. "I may do the same."

Easy for her to be amused. She wasn't the one being hunted.

IT WAS A WEIRD, unsettling day. Lindsay pretended to work more than actually accomplishing anything. Her ability to concentrate was shattered; like light bouncing off so many irregular fragments of glass, it was impossible to focus on one thing.

To start with, she couldn't slip quietly in from Sadie's office and go to work. Instead, the moment she appeared, the five caseworkers who happened to be at their desks all lifted their heads.

"Wow," Ashley Sheldon said. "I don't look *anything* like you, but I had to practically produce ID to prove I wasn't you." Ashley preened, as if anybody with eyes couldn't tell she was far prettier.

Or maybe Lindsay was just feeling sour.

"Yes, having the press hanging out in our parking lot is a nuisance," she said, without elaborating.

The newest hire, Jenn Armstrong, asked, "Is there anything you want us to say?" She flushed. "I mean, what *should* I say?"

"'No comment,'" Lindsay told her. "Just keep repeating it. I already reminded them that our work is kept confidential."

"Yeah, like that'll work," Matt Grudin sneered.

Unless she was imagining things, his gaze held acute dislike. Had she just never seen it before? He might have moved on from her refusal to go out with him, but did he hold a grudge?

She raised her eyebrows, refusing to look away. "Do you have a better suggestion?"

"Yeah, tell them to shove it up their—"

Before he finished, Gayle Schaefer, a quiet woman in her fifties, interrupted. "Sure. Sadie might have something to say about that."

Lindsay felt a physical relief when Matt turned his sneer toward the other woman.

"Then I'll tell her where she can go, too. I've started looking for another job anyway. I can hardly wait to get out of here."

Gayle shrugged and turned her attention back to her laptop.

Ray Hammond caught Lindsay's eyes and grimaced, his expression friendly.

She smiled back, but not so widely as to encourage him.

And then, having opened her laptop, she stared at

her screensaver and asked herself if any of her co-workers could be hiding enough rage to kill so ruth-lessly. Could someone so brutal be hiding behind an ordinary mask?

Jenn—no. Lindsay really hadn't gotten to know her, but she was straight out of grad school and had only worked here at CPS for six or seven months. She'd inherited Hank Cousins's caseload, but otherwise hadn't been assigned any of the heartbreaking cases. Of course, she could have grown up in some kind of sick situation and had plotted for years—four years for an undergraduate degree, another two to three for her master's—just so she could be in a position to punish every man like her father or uncle or whoever it was that hurt her. If so, she was the best actor Lindsay had ever seen. No, she wouldn't believe it.

Ashley Sheldon wasn't one of Lindsay's favorite coworkers; she could be a bitch. But Lindsay couldn't see her as a possible suspect, either. She was too self-centered. How would these murders help her?

On the flip side, she didn't seem to like Lindsay, either.

Gayle was quiet enough to hide a fuel tank full of rage, but Lindsay couldn't see it. Gayle was kind, efficient…and used a cane. She'd returned to CPS a year and a half ago after a several-year absence. Lindsay had been told that Gayle had multiple sclerosis and was currently in remission. If that was true, she wouldn't have been strong enough to overpower any of the four men.

Lindsay sneaked a look toward Matt Grudin, still at his desk typing furiously on his laptop. Updating his résumé, maybe. *He* was obviously angry, and some of that was directed her way. More than she'd realized, in fact. At about six feet, he was solidly built. Physically, he was capable, she thought. But if he were the killer, wouldn't he be trying *not* to gain attention?

Ray Hammond was more of an enigma to Lindsay, a handsome guy and a little too cocky for her tastes. That said, he seemed dedicated to his job and she'd seen him handling difficult people with ease and showing compassion to scared children. But who knew? He could be more burned out than was apparent.

That left the three coworkers not here at the moment, probably meeting with witnesses or family members. And she couldn't forget Sadie, who had worked in Child Protective Services longer than any of them, albeit not in this office, and who did still take on some investigations. Oh—and Celeste, of course, although that stretched credulity.

Work, Lindsay told herself, but five minutes later her mind had circled back to the beginning. Could Matt really hate her that much…?

She looked up from her laptop but again, as with every time she did, she found her coworkers surreptitiously watching her. Her eyes flew back down to her screen.

She thought her day couldn't get any worse. Untill Daniel—Detective Deperro—and Boyd Chaney, Granger County sheriff, showed up to escort her into the conference room again to interview her.

Chapter Eight

Thursday, Daniel parked at the curb two doors down from the Norris house. More accurately, from the house where Paige Norris would soon live alone if she didn't sell it. For the moment, yellow tape still stretched across the front door; Paige was staying in a hotel.

There were a few neighbors he had yet to catch at home. Some had apparently been away for the weekend, and unavailable the other times he'd knocked on their doors.

Today, Melinda was tied up with another investigation. Daniel had figured lunch hour might be a good time to find someone home who hadn't been at other times of the day.

With the sun high in the sky, the heat hit Daniel as soon as he stepped out of his unmarked SUV. This was one of those moments when he wished he didn't have air-conditioning in it, not to mention the police station and his home. The plunge from low to high temperatures was what got to him. He'd be sweat-soaked in no time.

What were the odds he'd learn anything at all helpful from random neighbors who hadn't thought to call 9-1-1 and say, *I saw this man carrying a bloody ax running out the back door?* Sure, and the witness also saw the make, color and model of the car the ax-wielder hopped into.

Daniel was not optimistic.

Here they were, nearly two weeks since the first murder, and they now had four bodies. And no leads. No witnesses. Nobody had heard anything, noticed an unfamiliar car in the vicinity. Nothing in the background of any CPS worker jumped out at him to justify formally interviewing him or her.

Monday, after he and Boyd had talked to Lindsay at the CPS offices, he'd managed to start casual conversations with Matt Grudin and Ray Hammond. A couple of the women had jumped in, too, but he'd focused on the men. Hadn't taken him thirty seconds to discover how intensely he disliked Grudin, but he knew he'd started with a bias. That said, the guy did carry a boatload of anger coupled with arrogance. The fact that most of his coworkers must know Lindsay had turned him down wasn't something he took lightly. He didn't succeed in hiding how pleased he was that Lindsay was in trouble, an attitude that shot him straight to the top of Daniel's list of suspects. Grudin ticked a lot of the markers Daniel was looking for.

Hammond maintained a bland facade that made him unreadable. Unremarkable, too, if Daniel hadn't known that he, too, had unsuccessfully pursued Lindsay.

His next stop had been to talk to the IT unit, who claimed there'd been no hacking of the database, and to Sadie Culver, who wasn't surprised at his interest in the caseworkers she directed but either didn't have so much as a nugget of suspicion toward any of them or chose not to share it.

After the interviews, he'd ruled out a couple of the women he didn't see as physically able to commit the murders. And he hadn't been able to narrow his interest in the others enough to justify going beyond background checks and some general questions about the caseworkers' schedules and whether any of them had been involved, even in a secondary role, with any of the CPS investigations that had ended in murder.

Although Melinda and Boyd were as baffled as he was, frustration didn't seem to ride them the way it did Daniel. Boyd was mostly peeved that a man like Howard Haycroft had slipped by the employment vetting at the ranch. Melinda's dark mood had to do with her determination to be the one to crack the case. Proving she was more competent, smarter, than Boyd Chaney was her reason for getting up in the morning, as far as Daniel could tell. She hadn't done or said anything so far that would compel him to issue a warning, but her simmering competitiveness irritated him.

Monday hadn't been improved by the gauntlet of journalists, some with TV cameras, he and Boyd had had to run to get into the state DHS offices to talk to

Lindsay. "We are not at this point prepared to make a statement" didn't even slow the shouted questions. Daniel hated knowing that it had to have been worse for her. He had called her several times during the week, ostensibly to ask additional questions of his own but really to find out how she was doing. Every time, the strain in her voice had been a reminder of her face during the Monday interview: too pale, the bones seemingly more prominent than usual, purple circles beneath her eyes.

He'd wanted to do a lot more than call her, but had reined himself in enough to know he needed to keep his distance. He shouldn't have taken her riding at his place that one time.

The week had passed with excruciating slowness. Now here he was on Thursday, waiting for the other shoe to drop.

Who was next to die?

Shaking his head, he rang a doorbell, stepping to one side of the door while he waited for a response. No, he didn't suppose the middle-aged man who resided at this address intended to whip out a shotgun and blast him through the door, but better safe than sorry.

To his mild surprise, he heard footsteps and a minute later the door opened.

Daniel held out his badge and elicited the information that this was the homeowner, Ralph Brown.

"Sir, I'd like to ask you a few questions." He nodded toward the Norris house. "I'm sure you heard about the murder."

"You kidding?" The guy stepped out on the porch and followed Daniel's gaze. He looked older than his years, his face weather beaten and heavily lined, his hair steel gray. "That's all anyone talks about. I only knew those folks to wave at, but it shakes you up."

"I understand. Is there any chance you were home between, say, eight-thirty and eleven in the morning that day? Might you have seen Mrs. Norris leave for work?"

"Yeah, I did. Real pretty woman. Always friendly."

Daniel smiled. "Yes, she is." *Allows her husband to sexually abuse her young daughters, but hey—she smiles at the neighbors.* "Did you see anyone arrive at the house, before or after she left?"

"No, I left probably twenty minutes after she did. I remember running a little late. I can't see their house from any of my windows, you know. It's blocked by my next-door neighbor's place. I only noticed Mrs. Norris because I happened to be looking out when she drove by."

"Yes, I understand. But, say, while you were backing out of your garage, or if you drove past their place…"

Ralph shook his head. "Only thing I remember was a car parked on the side street. Never seen it before, haven't seen it again."

Daniel determined that he wasn't a car guy. He said it was an older sedan, he thought a Toyota but couldn't be sure. He might have seen the symbol, but didn't Mazda or some other maker have a similar one? Car was white, but not real shiny. His eye had been caught because houses in the neighborhood all had double garages and driveways. Hardly anybody parked at the curb except guests when someone was holding a party.

After thanking him, Daniel walked back to his own vehicle. Back in the direct sun, he was barely conscious of being hammered by the heat. This wasn't a direct lead to a suspect, but at least he had something to go on. A white maybe-Toyota.

The driver could have easily slipped through the gate into the backyard and entered the house through the slider, if it hadn't been locked. It wasn't locked when Melinda found Norris dead.

Getting behind the wheel, waiting for his air-conditioning to kick in, he felt energized. He thought Ralph Brown had seen the killer's car.

It was a start.

BACK AT THE STATION, the first thing Daniel did was look to see what everyone working for Child Protective Services here in town drove. He wasn't really surprised to find that none of them drove a white sedan of any kind, much less a Toyota. That would have been too easy.

After some thought, he pulled up the list of vehicles stolen in the past month. He blinked when he came upon a Toyota Corolla, 2008, white. Researching it further, he learned it had not been recovered. It had gone missing seventeen days ago. Right timeline, if the killer had also driven it when he murdered Martin Ramsey.

The car's owner lived in an older neighborhood on Grouse Street, a few blocks from the business district. It had evidently belonged to the seventeen-year-old daughter. He called her and she told him she'd been leaving for her summer job at Dairy Queen when she'd discovered her car was no longer parked in its usual spot in the alley.

As a cop, Daniel wasn't a fan of alleys. They were too private. Backyards tended to be fenced. Garages accessed by the alley also blocked any view of it from the houses. Trash left out for pickup created great places to hide. In fact, alleys were perfect sites to commit just about any kind of crime and were cordially hated by CSIs.

He couldn't be certain this was the right car, but he thought the chances were good it was. He'd put out the word for patrol officers to sharpen their watch for it.

His desk phone rang, and he signed off with the teen and switched calls. "Deperro."

He allowed himself a fleeting moment of hope that this was about any other crime. He did have quite a few investigations gathering dust in stacks on his desk. When he recognized the voice of a lieutenant on the patrol side, that hope gained altitude.

"Detective? This is Griggs. We just received a call requesting a welfare check. Something the woman said got me thinking. I did a background check and found the man we're supposed to check on was involved in a nasty child abuse case a couple of years back. Name's Bradley Taubeneck. You want to ride along, just in case?"

Daniel resisted the temptation to thump his head on his desk. "I do." Because he loved finding mutilated bodies, he thought sardonically.

He drove himself, following a patrol unit, taking the opportunity to do some quick research. He didn't learn as much as he'd like. Taubeneck had been charged with child abuse, but those charges were later dismissed. Lot of backstory, Daniel was willing to bet.

The landscape west of town was dryer than out Daniel's way. Here, an occasional herd of cattle grazed on high desert scrub behind barbed wire fences. The patrol car turned onto a dirt track that led toward a distant house and barns. Daniel was soon enveloped in a dust cloud. He couldn't see a whole lot until they both parked behind the ranch house.

He knew the patrol officer Griggs had assigned to the welfare check, a guy about his age named Keith Shead. They greeted each other and walked to the back door. Shead knocked firmly, waited and did it again. No response. After a brief consulation, they separated to circle the house and meet in front.

Daniel saw no movement inside the uncovered windows of what appeared to be a bedroom and an empty room. At a third window, he went still, his hand sliding to the butt of his weapon. This, too, had been a bedroom but was now trashed. It was as if someone in a rage had thrown furniture against the walls. Even more cautiously, he moved forward, ducking to sneak a peek before rounding the corner. Shead waited for him on the front porch.

"See anything?" Shead asked in a low voice.

"Somebody threw a mighty big temper tantrum in one of the bedrooms. Looks like it was a little boy's room. A lot of fury there."

"Blinds were down on a couple of the windows, but the kitchen looked okay, just…empty. No remnants of a recent meal or anything like that."

Daniel nodded and rang the doorbell. A gong sounded from within. He pulled a latex glove from his pocket and put it on before trying the doorknob. Locked.

"We may have to break in, but let's try the outbuildings first."

Shead agreed, following Daniel back around so he could see the evidence of the epic temper tantrum.

Giving a low whistle, he said, "I wonder if that's recent or happened a long time ago."

Had Taubeneck lost his family? Crap. He wished he'd called Lindsay on the way.

In fact…

"Give me a minute," he said, and Shead nodded, walking toward their parked cars. Daniel dialed Lindsay's mobile number and waited through five rings before she answered, sounding tense.

"Detective?"

Forget being on a first-name basis. He was still in the doghouse.

"What can you tell me about Bradley Taubeneck?"

The silence that ensued raised the hairs on the back of his neck.

"Is he dead?"

"We're doing a welfare check. I'm told he was involved in a mess that brought CPS in." He frowned. "Were you the caseworker?"

"Of course I was." Her voice had lost all life, sounded numb. "You think you'll find him dead."

"That's a possibility I hope you'll keep to yourself for now."

"Yes."

"What happened to the child?"

"It was a little boy. He wasn't in his bed come morning. They…found him dead outside in the snow. Doors were locked."

He swore. "Did the father throw him out as punishment or something?"

"That's how it appeared at first. I ended up having some doubts about what really happened."

Daniel let another expletive slip out. With the weather currently so hot, how would a killer have replicated the poor boy's death? "Okay," he said after a minute. "I'll let you know what we find."

He and Shead stuck together to search, given that they didn't know what they were facing. Maybe the guy just wasn't answering his phone and would be hostile to have law enforcement officers prowling around his property.

The barn was a washout. Daniel did notice no animals were inside. He climbed the ladder to the hayloft, even moved a few bales to be sure a body wasn't wedged behind them. Shaking his head, he dropped back to the barn floor.

Another outbuilding held farm equipment: a tractor and more. The last one, closest to the house, had buckets, some tools and a white appliance it took him a second to recognize. A chest freezer. His gaze arrowed in on a hasp that had not been original…and the closed, heavy-duty padlock.

As if there was any doubt, a metal bucket filled with ashes sat right in front of the freezer.

Shead was the one swearing up a storm now. He ran back to the other outbuilding and returned fast and sweating, bolt cutters in hand. Daniel doubted speed was going to accomplish anything now. The ashes in the bucket were cool.

The padlock didn't want to surrender. They took turns, untill finally it snapped in two and Daniel wrenched it off, lifted the hasp and pushed open the top.

With ice crystalized over his eyes, nostrils and mouth, the man inside was very dead.

"I'M SORRY," SADIE SAID, her expression sympathetic. "You know this isn't punishment, and I don't believe for a second that you played any part in these murders. I hope you understand that I just can't let you near a case until this is cleared up."

Lindsay wouldn't touch a new investigation with a ten-foot pole. But to be blocked even from working on ongoing cases came as a shock, despite the fact that she'd tried to prepare herself for this outcome. Once details about the latest murder topped local television news broadcasts, Sadie probably hadn't felt she had any choice. The news of the most recent murder had spread like wildfire on social media even before news sources had picked it up.

While Lindsay understood where Sadie was coming from, she was still furious. Not at Sadie; in her shoes, Lindsay would have made the same decision. No, most of her anger was directed at the killer, who seemed determined to destroy her career if not her life even if he didn't add her to his murder tally. But she had plenty of anger left over, simmering beneath the surface, choking her.

She nodded and rose to her feet. "I'll clean out my desk."

She'd almost escaped her supervisor's office when Sadie said from behind her, in what was presumably meant to be encouragement, "You'll be back at work before you know it."

Sure she would. Lindsay didn't even pause. Feeling the heat of humiliation and anger in her cheeks, she marched into the large space occupied by her fellow caseworkers, trying not to make eye contact with anyone. Of course, silence fell at her appearance.

Sitting down at her desk, she wished she had a box, then thought, *Do I really have anything here I really value?* The answer was no.

She opened her already hefty handbag and shoved a few things in. A framed photo of her last foster mom. Two paperback books. A handful of energy bars that might go stale before she made it back—if she ever did.

She was already carrying her laptop. After opening and closing the final drawers, staring in and seeing nothing but the detritus of work she'd allowed to become her entire life, she stood abruptly enough to send her desk chair rolling back.

For the first time, she let herself notice the gaping stares of every single caseworker here in the office.

And her anger rolled over her until she literally saw red.

"Yes," she said loudly, "there's been another murder. I've been suspended, in case you're wondering." Without fault, but that wasn't the point. She looked from face to face. "It would appear that somebody expects me to be pleased because he's making child abusers suffer the same pain their victims did. He's punishing them the way he must think they should have been punished in the first place. The way I failed to do, with my silly insistence on following the letter of the law." Her voice continued rising as her grip on any self-control slipped. She should shut her mouth and leave…but why? she thought recklessly. *I have an audience. The perfect audience.*

One that might well include a serial killer.

"Well, you know what?" She turned in a slow circle to take in everyone in the room. "I'm *not* pleased. I'm enraged. Who does this person think he is, to sit in judgment on people he's never even met? People who haven't been convicted of a crime?" In fact, most of the murder victims hadn't been. Not yet, anyway. "You know he cold-bloodedly murdered a very young man only because, when he was a kid himself, he defended his father?"

They all gazed at her, rapt, unblinking. Movement

caught out of the corner of her eye told her Sadie had appeared. And, oh Lord, was that Glenn behind her?

Well, right this minute, she didn't care.

"The latest victim—" Her voice broke. "From almost the beginning, I've believed he was innocent of the accusations. I was responsible for the charges being dropped, although his wife left him and took his other child with her. But this time, the arrogant monster who has named himself judge and executioner murdered *an innocent man*. Think about that."

She slung her laptop over her shoulder and grabbed her handbag. "Maybe I'm no better person than he is, because I hope he—or she," Lindsay added, again glaring from face to face, "suffers the same agony he's inflicted on other people. The difference between us? Unlike this sick creep, I won't be taking justice in my own hands."

She noted the ducked heads, the eyes that no longer wanted to meet hers. Did everyone in this room guess they were under suspicion, because they were among the very few people who had access to the details of the original abuse cases?

She opened her mouth again but regained enough self-control to do nothing but shake her head and stomp toward the exit. Sadie and Glenn stepped hastily aside before she could knock them out of her way. Seconds later, she was out in the heat of the day and pulling open her car door.

"Lindsay."

Recognizing the voice, she closed her eyes and her shoulders sagged. She hated knowing how disappointed Glenn would be in her for making such a spectacular scene. She couldn't even say she felt better for having vented.

I can't go back to work with those same people.

She tossed the two bags onto the passenger seat and turned to face the man who'd given her so much support and encouragement.

"Bet you didn't know I had it in me," she said wryly.

Astonishingly, his smile was as kind as ever, his presence as steadying. He had the same quality Daniel Deperro did, she was surprised to realize, one that made her want to believe, deep inside, that he wouldn't let her down. It wasn't just physical, although like Daniel he was solidly built. Well, not counting the roll around the middle he'd been acquiring since his retirement.

Although she liked and admired Glenn, she was disturbed to realize she had never let herself absolutely, 100 percent, believe she could trust and depend on him. She wouldn't be able to where Daniel was concerned, either. Some scars ran deep.

"'Course I knew you did," he said, his brown eyes compassionate. "You always had a fire. That's what this job takes."

"Uh-huh."

"I know how much stress you've been under. I'm sorry I haven't called."

"I didn't expect you to. It's just…been strange. You know? Why me?"

"Maybe because you've been given the toughest

cases from the beginning," he suggested. "Somebody admires you."

"Or resents me."

He waggled a hand. "Possible, I suppose."

"I'll be okay." She forced a smile and rose on tiptoe to kiss his cheek. "It's about time I took a vacation, anyway."

He laughed, kissed her cheek in turn and said, "This *is* a paid break?"

"Yep." This second smile came more easily. "Maybe I should take an Alaska cruise, escape the heat."

"Go for it." He hesitated. "I'm just sorry you don't have a partner to go with you."

Suddenly curious, she asked, "Have you ever been married?" He'd been single as long as she'd known him.

"Sure. Divorced." He grimaced. "Job can do that to you."

"Job can keep you single, too," Lindsay said in exactly the same tone.

Then she saw someone else emerge from the state offices and start across the parking lot in her direction. Matt Grudin. Maybe he intended to be supportive, too…or maybe he thought she'd be vulnerable right now and he could get her in bed. Eager to avoid him, she said hurriedly, "I need to go, Glenn. Talk to you later."

He glanced over his shoulder and turned back with his bushy gray eyebrows high. "Grudin, huh?"

"Just don't want to talk to anyone. Except you," she added hurriedly.

He contemplated her for a minute, then nodded and stepped back. "Better step on it."

She hopped into her roasting hot car, started the engine and, uselessly, the air-conditioning and pulled out of the parking slot before Matt reached Glenn's side.

As she drove away, she didn't look in the rearview mirror even once.

Chapter Nine

Daniel's hands clenched and unclenched on the steering wheel as he drove from the police station to Lindsay's house. She couldn't call and tell him she'd been suspended from her job?

The call from her supervisor, Sadie Culver, had come out of the blue, catching him just as he was leaving to go home. She seemed like a nice lady and had sounded apologetic.

"I think everybody was gaping at her, like drivers do an accident on the highway, and she blew her top. Told them all she didn't think for a minute that knocking off child abusers was a good thing. Said the killer was monster and a sick creep. Glenn was here and followed her out to be sure she was okay, but I still thought you'd want to know."

Yes, he did. And he sure as hell didn't believe she was "okay." As deeply committed to her job as Lindsay was, she had to be feeling lost. Pissed, too, obviously, which he understood.

If she wasn't home... He didn't know what he'd do. Wait? Come back later? She'd had all day; who knew, maybe she'd thrown some bags in her car and taken off, the way she'd planned the Saturday he'd talked her into horseback riding with him instead.

But he saw her car in the driveway as soon as he turned onto her block. Now he just had to hope she didn't ignore his knock on the door, always a possibility given their occasionally adversarial relationship.

He parked in her driveway, blocking her car in. Not likely she'd feel like going out tonight, anyway, unless she had girlfriends who'd insist on dragging her out to a bar. He didn't believe that, though; he couldn't be mistaken about her quality of aloneness.

Daniel strode up to the porch and leaned on the doorbell. He was just about ready to do it again when he heard movement inside. She opened the door and gazed at him without any visible emotion.

"What can I do for you, Detective?" she asked after a minute.

"I heard you were suspended."

"Who told you?"

"Your boss." He hesitated. "I think she was worried about you."

"Because I ranted and raved."

"Yeah, that was probably it." He nodded toward the door opening. "Can I come in?"

She gave it some thought but finally said, "I suppose," and backed up.

Until then, he'd kept his gaze above her shoulders, but now he couldn't resist a look at her spectacular legs revealed beneath cutoff shorts. He liked the effect of the body-clinging tank top, too. She was fine-boned but had ample curves. They were on display right now, which might be one reason she had been reluctant to open the door to him.

"You alone?" he asked, stepping in.

"Yes. I just poured myself a glass of white wine. Can I interest you in one?"

Daniel wasn't much of a wine drinker, but he said, "Sure, why not. I'm off the clock."

Her solitary glass of wine sat on an antique kitchen table, so he pulled up a chair opposite it.

Her feet were bare, too, he noticed while she was pouring another glass and putting the wine back in the fridge. Narrow feet, long toes. He moved a little uncomfortably as his gaze traveled upward.

She turned just then and caught him looking. Her eyes narrowed, but she set the wine down in front of him and plopped into a chair without comment.

"What? Did you imagine I'm suicidal, and you had to rush to the rescue?"

He smiled. "Not for a minute. You're tougher than that."

"Yes, I am." She stared at him with defiance, just long enough to make her point, but then she lifted one shoulder and her mouth twisted. "Crappy day, though."

"Yeah." He had to clear his throat. Somehow, he saw looking down, he'd reached across the table and covered her hand with his. "Told everyone how you really feel, huh?"

She didn't turn her hand over to clasp his, but she

didn't pull away, either. "Did Sadie tell you what I said?"

"More or less. I want to hear about it from you." He wished she hadn't made herself a target if the killer had happened to be there when she let loose. But he also understood that Lindsay wasn't much for pretending. Her directness was one of many qualities that attracted him. As a cop, he sometimes thought he heard nothing but lies all day, every day.

So she told him, possibly verbatim, what she'd said before stalking out of work.

Daniel snagged on the last part. "You're sure this Bradley Taubeneck didn't lock his kid out of the house that night?"

Vivid blue eyes haunted by memories met his. "Without a doubt? No. But... I'm pretty sure. I had suspicions I couldn't prove, so I left them out of the file. His wife accused him, and it was really unlikely the kid slipped out of the house and got locked out accidentally. Of course that happens, though. If the parents locked up and didn't bother to check on their kids before they went to bed."

"What did they say when you asked?"

"The mother claimed she had a migraine."

"But you didn't believe her," he said slowly.

"At first I bought into her story. She was weepy, grieving, even as she darted accusing looks at her husband." Her eyes appeared unfocused now. "Because of her headache, he was bearing more of the childcare responsibilities than usual, and Max was being really loud and wild. They were starting to wonder if he might be hyperactive. Anyway, the more I spoke with them, the more I saw genuine shock and bewilderment and grief on the dad's part and something a little off on hers. He seemed…stunned that she'd point a finger at him. Once he started to say, 'You know I'm always patient with Max. It's you who—' He didn't finish the sentence, but he didn't have to." She sighed and took a swallow of the wine. "It was the kind of investigation I hate the most. They didn't have any near neighbors, which meant no witnesses."

"Plus, Max couldn't have gone to a neighbor's."

"Right." Lindsay shrugged. "I convinced the DA to drop the charges, but I couldn't prove Bradley was innocent any more than I was able to prove his wife was the one who lost it with her own kid."

"Did people you worked with know about your doubts?"

She frowned. "I'm sure I expressed some concern, but they may have thought I had to let him off because there was no way to be sure what happened."

Daniel swore and rubbed a hand over his face. "So our killer thinks Bradley was guilty as hell and got off scot-free." More slowly, he said, "Or, I guess I should say, he *thought* Bradley was guilty." After an even longer pause, he added, "Or else he doesn't care one way or the other. The victims are just…symbols."

"That's even more sickening."

He looked away for a minute. "Yeah."

Sounding stricken, Lindsay said, "You really think somebody at CPS is doing this."

"You have any better ideas?"

She shook her head, gazing into her wineglass as if she'd find answers there.

"Can you tell me who was there to hear your blowup?"

She explained that it had been early enough in the morning, only three coworkers had been missing: Ashley Sheldon, Gayle Schaefer and Ray Hammond. "Well," she said, "I'm sure Celeste heard every word out at reception, too, and so did Sadie—I guess you already knew that—and Glenn Wilson, my last supervisor."

Daniel frowned. "What was he doing there?"

"He pops in once a week or so, just kind of keeping a read on our emotional stability, I guess you could say. Truthfully, I think he's bored."

"Ms. Culver doesn't mind? She doesn't feel like he's looking over her shoulder?"

"No, she says that when she first started, he was really generous when she had questions. I've seen them go out for coffee together, even."

"Does he still have access to the database?"

Her surprise was obvious. "Of course not! You aren't thinking *he* could be—"

"It's going to turn out to be somebody you know, Lindsay."

"Lovely thought."

They looked at each other in silence for what had to be a minute. Damn, she was beautiful. He wanted to stand up, go around the table and pull her to her feet. Hold her—although he was too likely to kiss her once she was in his arms.

What he ought to do was go home. Daniel already knew he wouldn't be doing that. Not until he had no other choice.

"Listen," he said, "what if I order a pizza? Or that Thai place delivers."

Her chin lifted in an all-too familiar gesture of independence. "I'm okay by myself. Don't feel you have to stay to, I don't know, prop me up."

"I want to stay."

She searched his face again, finally nodding. "Then pizza sounds good. Can I have my half veggie?"

"You don't eat meat?"

"Sometimes. It just sounds good. Less greasy."

"Works for me, too." He had the number in his phone and dialed immediately. While he was talking to some kid at the pizza joint, her phone rang. He turned to see her eyeing the caller's number with puzzlement.

She answered anyway. "Hello?"

Color drained from her face.

"'I THOUGHT YOU, of all people, would understand.'"

Daniel crouched next to her chair at the table. "That's all he said?"

"No. Then he said, 'It's not like *you've* never made a mistake.' It was a whisper." Lindsay's voice shook. So did her hand, she saw distantly, as she reached for her wineglass. "I think it was a man, but I'm not positive."

"Damn."

"Damn?" That suddenly struck her as almost funny. "A serial killer knows my phone number? He thought *I'd* understand? 'Damn' doesn't seem to cover it." She shuddered.

"I know some worse words."

His eyes were steady on her face, but sharp, too, as if seeing more than she wanted to give away. One of his big, warm hands rested on her thigh, the other on her lower back. His touch felt so good, it took all she had to hold her spine straight, refuse to succumb to such temptation.

"Not sure those words would help," he added.

"No."

"Lindsay, you know you have to tell me what he meant about you making mistakes."

She shook her head. "I don't know. Truly. I think we're all afraid a child will die because we didn't act or maybe thought counseling would be enough. Or didn't do an adequate background check, like me with Martin Ramsey. As bad in a different way would be taking a child from a parent who was innocent but you hadn't done a thorough enough investigation. Bradley Taubeneck is an example of someone who suffered even though we *didn't* charge him."

Daniel's knees must hurt, as long as he'd crouched there beside her, but he didn't move. "Maybe that's the kind of thing this guy thinks was a 'mistake.' You didn't nail the guy when you had the chance."

She shivered. "So he took care of it."

"Yeah."

She went for what had to be a pathetic smile. "Did you get the pizza ordered?"

"Yeah." The expression on his angular face hardened, and he rose to his feet, looking down at her. "You're too vulnerable here. I think it really is time for a vacation, preferably far, far away. A cruise. Norwegian fjords. The Caribbean. Even Alaska would do for the short-term."

For a moment she imagined it. She'd lie back on a deck chair and sip some fruity drink to try to mute her worries. Dolphins would frolic beside the ship. She wouldn't turn on her phone at all. She'd go to glitzy shows every night, stuff her face, read all the books she never found time to get to.

Assuming she could concentrate, what with the fruity drinks and the fear gnawing at her belly and constricting her heart.

"I can't," she heard herself blurt before she'd really made a decision. "I'm in the middle of this. You know I am."

"I want to take you out of the middle." He looked and sounded grim.

"I know. I understand. It's just…none of it is my fault, but I still feel responsible, in a way." She held up a hand to stop the comeback rising to his lips. "No, listen. Somehow, I must have given the impression that I wished abusers would die. Of course, it's not something *I* can do, but I must have given off the idea that I wouldn't mind if someone else did it for me."

Daniel swore. "Have you ever felt that way?"

She swallowed. "As mad as I sometimes get, no. No. But maybe I complained too much. All I know is that I can't run away now. It's better if he focuses on *me* instead of…whoever he might already be stalking."

He swung away, paced the length of the kitchen then back, his expression dark. "You infuriated him today. He can't kid himself anymore that you're secretly grateful to him for having the guts to do what no one else will, that you'd throw yourself into his arms in gratitude if he revealed himself to you."

The idea made Lindsay's stomach lurch. "I know," she said softly. Her fingernails bit into her palms.

"You saw one of the bodies. You think you know what he's capable of, but you don't," he said harshly. "*Monster* is the right word for him. Can you imagine finding yourself locked in a freezer? It's dark and hopeless and you get colder and colder until ice forms in your nostrils and eyes and lungs?" He planted his hands on the table and bent forward, eyes dark and boring into hers. "How do you think he'd kill *you*, Lindsay, now that you've violated his worldview?"

Her throat closed. Her teeth wanted to chatter.

"What is it you think you can do by staying in town?"

"I…" He was right, in a way. She had no idea why she felt such certainty. Was she trying to prove something to herself? "Maybe he'll stop now, since he knows it's not what I want."

Daniel's laugh was incredulous. "Get real. *You*

were only peripheral. Nobody does what he has been doing unless they enjoy it. He's had more than a taste now. He'll keep killing. If you were one of his victims—" He shook his head and turned his back.

Suddenly angry, she said, "Do I stay away forever? How are you going to catch him? If he does focus on me, that might give you a chance."

A growled obscenity expressed his opinion of that as he turned back to glare at her. "If I thought I could get away with it, I'd take you into protective custody."

"You wouldn't."

"No, but by God you aren't going to be alone for a minute from now on. Do you hear me?"

"Isn't that protective custody?"

"The kind that doesn't involve a jail cell. Count your blessings."

She did. A sudden realization of how petrified she'd be if he walked out on her cracked the wall that she hid behind. She hadn't needed anyone since she was a child, but now she needed this man, and not only to keep her safe.

"I'll definitely count my blessings," she managed.

His expression changed. Whatever she saw on his face was unfamiliar, made her weak, vulnerable.

"Damn it, Lindsay." He wrapped his hands around her upper arms and lifted her to her feet. "Do you know how much I want to kiss you?"

Panicked, she shook her head. Sex, she could do. But with Daniel, it would be more, and she didn't dare.

He muttered something she couldn't make out and

pulled her close, tucked her head against his shoulder and held her against him. His body radiated heat. For an instant, she stood stiffly, fighting against the pure seduction of powerful arms, hard thighs and a muscular chest. Then a hitch of breath escaped her and she couldn't do anything but wrap her arms around his torso and quiver with tension even as she tried to soak in some of his strength.

"You'll be okay," he murmured in her ear. "We'll catch this vile excuse for a human being. I swear we will."

Lindsay actually believed him. She might not later, when she was alone in bed, but right now, she did. Her head bobbed. At least she wasn't crying.

He rubbed his cheek on her hair, or maybe it was his lips. If she lifted her face to his...

No, no, no! What a horrible time to start anything with him. It was classic; little woman desperate to please the man who gave her the best chance of survival. Later...maybe. Now, she breathed in his scent and gathered herself to pull away.

DANIEL LAY STRETCHED out on Lindsay's sleeper sofa, which was both too short for him and ribbed with what felt like steel girders. He'd given up trying to find a comfortable position; there wasn't one.

Hell, he couldn't sleep anyway. Either he was thinking about how to catch this killer, or he brooded about Lindsay. In between, he remembered how she'd felt in his arms, actually allowing herself a minute or two of human contact, of physical support. Probably just as well she'd retreated when she did, because he'd been getting aroused and she'd have noticed any moment. He loved every lush curve on her body along with the taut muscles and a strength so much a part of her; he worried about why she was so wary of him, not to mention every other man. Maybe women, too. The concept of trust didn't seem to be in her frame of reference. Her kind of strength was born out of necessity.

He clasped his hands behind his head and stared up at the dark ceiling. He could be patient. He thought he'd made some inroads already. Tonight, she'd clutched him with fierce strength. She'd let him hold her hand. The situation gave him some proximity, too. Harder for her to resist him when they were all but living together.

Any satisfaction sank under the weight of the real-life situation. He had a deeply bad feeling about that whispered reprimand from the killer. Lindsay was right to be scared that he had her personal phone number—and the confirmation that part of his motivation had been pleasing her. No surprise, Daniel had confirmed that the killer had called from a burner phone, probably already in a dumpster.

Would he come after her? Daniel considered the possibility realistic enough that he intended to provide protection for her twenty-four-seven. Tomorrow, he'd talk to his lieutenant and the police chief if necessary. In the meantime, he had already lined up Melinda to stay with her tomorrow, although it was the detective's day off. As dedicated as she was to her job, she hadn't seemed to mind. He'd spend nights here. He couldn't opt out of a callout, but he'd worry about it when it came. If he had to, he'd take Lindsay with him. Maybe drop her at one of his other cop friends' houses. They'd manage.

She obviously had some idea of being bait, but that wasn't happening unless he could come up with a foolproof plan. Something else to worry about tomorrow.

He listened hard, but heard only sounds that ought to be there. A car passing several blocks away, the refrigerator humming, the gurgle of the toilet flushing down the hall.

Apparently he wasn't the only one who was having trouble sleeping.

He lay rigid, listening for footsteps, but he heard nothing until a faint creaking told him she'd crawled back into bed.

Daniel groaned, wishing he was in that bed with her.

LINDSAY HADN'T FALLEN asleep until at least four in the morning. There was so much to think about, from the whispering, angry caller to the fact that Daniel was there, and not because he had an urgent need for answers. That thought warmed her. Still, she circled on to her state of unemployment, and then back to Daniel staying the night so she didn't have to be alone. Around and around and around…until she dropped into a deep, dark hole and didn't surface until strong beams of sunlight made their way into the room through the window blinds.

Blinking, she focused on the clock. 10:23. She couldn't remember the last time she'd slept so late.

After showering and dressing, she found a cop in her kitchen, just not the same one who'd slept on the sofa last night. Melinda McIntosh perched on a tall stool at the island, a laptop open in front of her.

Melinda lifted her head. "Good morning. Coffee's ready."

"Thank heavens." Lindsay poured a cup for herself and refilled Melinda's. "Don't you ever have a day off?" This *was* Saturday.

"I'd have been working no matter what. I can't turn my mind off."

Heartfelt, Lindsay said, "I know what you mean." They weren't the only ones, either; she doubted Daniel had gone home to laze around. Had he taken a full day off since the first murder?

Silly question.

"Daniel mentioned this Glenn Wilson," Melinda remarked.

"It can't be him. But I've been thinking. Do you know how many retired caseworkers, or ones who switched to another job, are still in the area?"

Melinda set down her mug with a click. "No. Do you?"

"I don't, but I've run into several. I saw…" She frowned. "Oh, why can't I remember his name?" She pondered. "Barry. Barry… Hill, that's it. Anyway, we talked for a minute in the produce department at

Safeway. That was probably two months ago, but I know he's still here."

"I'll request the names of caseworkers who have left in the last couple of years."

"Why just the last—oh." Duh. "Because they have to have known me."

"Right. Think back, will you? Who did you get along with? Have friction with? Any strange interactions?"

The questions kept coming. Had she ever dated a colleague? Had anyone besides Matt Grudin and Ray Hammond—Melinda had to glance at notes on her laptop for those names—ever seemed interested in her? Did she have a close friend among the current coworkers? In the past? Had anybody in particular ever expressed the wish that abusers suffer like their victims had?

That one had Lindsay making a face. "I imagine almost everyone has in a bad moment. Plus, we indulge in a lot of black humor when nobody else can hear."

Melinda sighed. "We do, too. Cops, I mean. All first responders, and I guess you're close to being one."

"I never thought of it that way, but yes."

Lindsay toasted a bagel for breakfast and then made them both sandwiches when lunchtime rolled around. In fact, while they talked, she started baking. Pumpkin bread first, then oatmeal raisin cookies.

"I have to do something or I'll go crazy," she admitted.

When would she get to run again? Do anything by herself? Maybe Daniel—or one of her babysitters—would take her to the gym where she could use a treadmill.

He called midafternoon, speaking first to Melinda and then Lindsay. Lucky she hadn't expected tender concern for her welfare.

"I've been thinking it might be possible for us to be proactive," he said when she came to the phone. "Do any cases you've handled stand out in your memory?"

Horrible thought.

"Lots of them." Clutching her phone, she closed her eyes. "But you mean ones where the abuser appears to have gotten off lighter than was justified?"

"Yeah." Daniel's deep voice had become gentle. "That's what I'm thinking."

A couple came to mind, one in particular where she'd *known*, with bone-deep certainty, that the mother had smothered the baby she hadn't wanted. Lindsay had never been able to prove it, though, and the autopsy didn't provide the conclusive results needed to try the woman in court.

"I wonder if he'd kill a woman," she said.

The silence told her what Daniel was thinking. A shiver crawled up her spine. *She* was a woman...and he wouldn't be guarding her around the clock if he weren't very much afraid that this killer intended to punish her, too.

Chapter Ten

The ringing phone jolted Daniel out of a typically maddening, surreal dream that ratcheted up his frustration. He sat up, for a fleeting instant unsure where he was, why the nightstand with his weapon and phone wasn't where it should be.

Then the phone rang again, and it all came back to him. Lindsay's sofa. Four more days of investigative dead ends. Four more nights at her place, struggling to keep his hands off her.

He fumbled for the phone. Damn, it was almost three in the morning. Good news never came in the middle of the night.

"Yeah," he answered huskily. "This is Deperro."

"Detective. Sorry to get you at this hour, but I had to tell you that you were right. As you know, the Mehnert woman blew me off when I talked to her the other day. Her baby died tragically. It was a travesty that Child Protective Services came after her. Even *they* had to admit they were wrong, so why would we think for a minute that some crazy vigilante would come after her, an innocent, heartbroken mother?"

Daniel had recognized the voice right away. It belonged to Detective Lee Nakamoto of the Washington County Sheriff's Department. Daniel had traced the woman Lindsay told her about to an address just outside Portland, Oregon, and contacted Nakamoto. The Mehnert woman had been Danica Lashbrook when Lindsay investigated her after the death of her two-month-old child. Turned out, she and her husband split barely a month later. The guy had probably shared Lindsay's suspicions. She'd remarried less than a year later and had taken up residence in western Oregon.

Nakamoto had agreed to go talk to her, tell her what had been happening in Sadler, suggest this would be a good time for her to make herself unavailable for a while. The woman had pretended shock. The detective had a feeling husband number two hadn't known anything about the CPS investigation. They'd had no child yet in the new marriage.

"She dead?" Daniel asked.

"Oh, yeah. Husband travels for his job. Got a late flight from San Francisco instead of spending another night the way he'd planned. He found Danica dead in bed."

"Let me guess. Smothered."

"Pillow over her face," Nakamoto agreed. "The ME may have more to say, but that's what it was set up to look like."

Daniel swore and scrubbed a hand over his scalp. "Keep me informed, will you? I'll try to determine if anyone on our list was out of town yesterday afternoon. Trouble is…"

"It's not that long a drive. Yeah."

"This is the sixth murder, and that's assuming we know about all of them."

"Clearly, he's willing to travel."

"How'd he get in the house?"

"Broke the pane on the kitchen door. Reached in to turn the dead bolt."

Daniel didn't need to comment on how ludicrous it was to put a dead bolt on a door with an easily shattered pane of glass. Why lock it at all?

He turned his head sharply when he caught movement out of the corner of his eye. Watching him and undoubtedly listening to his side of the conversation, Lindsay stood in the kitchen doorway, wearing what was essentially a long T-shirt with a cartoon cat on front. She hugged herself, and he saw that her toes were curled. From cold or shock? How much had she heard?

He and the other detective wound up the conversation and Daniel set his phone down on the table beside his holster and gun. He hadn't bothered to pull the bed part out last night. The couch definitely wasn't long enough for him, but the cushions were reasonably comfortable. Now, he patted the cushion beside him.

"Hey. Come here."

Her hesitation was brief, although he suspected she was being made shy by the sight of his bare chest. Then she came, sitting down with one leg curled under her so that she faced him, carefully keeping her gaze on his face.

"Someone's dead," she said.

"Danica Lashbrook."

"But you warned her."

"Yes. The local cops did at my request."

Her expression somber, Lindsay seemed to be struck by a memory. "She was really calculating. She'd turn this weepy, big-eyed look on her husband, a 'why are they treating me this way?' look, then turn to me with a dignified expression but with her lower lip trembling. But in between, I'd see flashes of anger or coldness. She thought she could get away with killing her baby, and she did."

"But not for long."

"No." Her gaze had turned inward. "I really detested her."

"Are you saying you understand our killer's motivation?"

"How can I not?" she responded with devastating honesty. "But I wanted to see her behind bars, not dead."

Daniel reached for her hand, exclaiming when he found it icy. "For God's sake!" The air-conditioning must have been running all night. He captured her other hand, too, determined to share his warmth. If she noticed, she didn't look down.

"How will you ever catch him?" she asked.

"If he doesn't make a mistake—and everyone does sooner or later—one of us will make an intuitive leap, or we'll just get lucky. There are cases that go cold, but in a county like this where we don't get that much murder, they're the minority."

Lindsay searched his face. Daniel didn't have a clue what she was thinking.

"I should go back to bed," she said, but didn't move.

"Lindsay—" He didn't know if it was smart or incredibly stupid, but his self-control had been crumbling by the day. He went with his impulse, gently tugging her forward.

Initially, she stayed stiff, her unfathomable gaze never wavering, but then she scooted closer. Daniel did his best to suppress his urgency as he brushed her lips with his, came back to savor them, finally dampening the seam of her lips with his tongue.

She made a funny little sound as she rose to her knees and wrapped her arms around his neck. With a groan, he lifted her onto his lap so that she straddled his hips.

Against her mouth, he mumbled, "Do you have any idea how hard it's been keeping my hands to myself?"

Lindsay pulled back enough for him to see her tiny smile. "I suspected." She rocked her hips, and he groaned again.

"I want you."

"I need you tonight," she whispered, and they came together in an inflammatory kiss that put an end to all qualms, all pretense.

SHE'D NEVER FELT anything like this. It was like being hit by a tsunami, so powerful she couldn't have broken free. His tongue thrust into her mouth, and she stroked it with her own. His hair was thick silk, her fingers tangled in it. One of his big hands gripped her hip to pace her involuntary rocking. The other moved restlessly, exploring her back, the nape of her neck, sliding around to cup one breast.

He started to roll her beneath him but checked himself.

"No. Bed," he said roughly, and straightened with her in his arms.

Lindsay locked her legs around his waist, grabbing hold of his powerful shoulders for more security. Yet as he strode down the hall, he carried her as if she weighed next to nothing. He knew which room was hers; every night, when she headed for bed, she'd been aware of his heated gaze following her.

After being awakened earlier by the ring of his phone and the deep, low sound of his voice, she'd thrown aside the covers when she got up. Now, he let her slide down his body until her feet touched the floor. Within seconds, he'd pulled the long T-shirt she wore over her head.

Voice thick, he said, "You're beautiful."

If anyone here was beautiful, it was him. She explored the sleek brown skin stretched over amazing muscles with her splayed hands. His hands, in turn, lifted her breasts, gently squeezed them, his palms rubbing her taut nipples.

Next thing she knew, she was on her back and he was suckling one of her breasts. She whimpered and arched, fingertips digging into his shoulders. Lindsay found she had no patience. She urged him on, her hips pushing up, seeking.

When Daniel lifted his head, she was glad for the light from the bedside lamp so that she could see his face, transformed by passion. The skin seemed to stretch tighter than usual over the strong bones, and his eyes had the hot gleam that had so tempted her all those nights when she'd known what he was thinking.

"Please" she heard herself beg.

He groaned again and said, "Hell. Give me a minute."

A minute? He walked out of the bedroom, leaving her incredulous. Only when he returned, something in his hand, did she understand he'd gone to the living room for a condom. Condoms plural, she saw, as he dropped several on the bedside stand.

He was magnificent in stretch boxer briefs, but he shed them in an instant and climbed into bed with her. She felt so desperate, she didn't care that he didn't give her any more chance to explore his body. She parted her legs and welcomed him.

She whimpered at the first pressure, unable to look away from his piercing dark eyes. Her fingernails dug into his back. How could she feel so much so fast? His weight on her, the way he filled her, the rhythm that was somehow just right, meant release came with stunning speed, dragging him with her. He rolled to one side, gathered her close and mumbled, "Damn."

Was that good or bad? It sounded as if he was as stunned as she felt. Lindsay wasn't sure she could move and didn't want to. She hardly knew what was happening to her.

Why him? She'd never been drawn to the kind of domineering man who assumed his orders would be obeyed instantly. Except that wasn't totally fair; Daniel Deperro, she had come to realize, was a complex, intelligent man capable of compassion and kindness. And passion that had overwhelmed her.

Giving a heavy sigh, he let her go and got out of bed. To return to the sofa, now that he'd had what he wanted? she wondered, stung. But he disappeared into the bathroom and returned less than a minute later. Of course he was coming back to bed. Lindsay didn't understand her volatile emotions. This wasn't like her.

But then, she'd never known anyone who had been murdered, never mind six victims now. She'd never known a killer before, or annoyed one. She'd never been fired or suspended from a job for any reason. And she'd never had a cop move in with her because he was afraid for her, either.

Live and learn.

Daniel's expression was harder to read now, as he gazed down at her for a minute before slipping beneath the covers as if this was where he belonged, reaching out a long arm to turn off the lamp and pulling her back to snuggle against him.

"Sleep," he said, his voice a soft rumble against her ear.

To her astonishment, she did.

HE MADE LOVE to her once more during the night and wanted to do it again when he awakened to early light. This time, though, she had curled away from him and slept so deeply, he didn't allow himself to wake her up at—he looked past her to the digital clock. 5:43. Good God. Why was *he* awake?

He'd been going to bed earlier since he'd come to stay at Lindsay's, though, and getting up earlier, too. This morning, he had even more to think about than usual. He lay still for a long time, looking at the back of her head, the silky mass of her hair, the tight curl of her body, and felt an echo of last night's shock.

Would she be annoyed or hurt that he hadn't managed to say the kind of thing a man probably should? "Damn" could be appreciative, or not. She hadn't said a single word, but she might have been waiting for him. Or she could be as shaken as he was.

He'd wanted her from first sight, but hadn't been sure he even liked her. For God's sake, he'd suspected her of murder! Lindsay wouldn't have forgotten that.

What was he doing here anyway? Last night's murder suggested the killer's focus remained on the abusive parents. Maybe he still believed Lindsay would swing around to his way of seeing things. In the days since the ominous phone call, Daniel hadn't seen even a hint that someone was watching her or the house. There'd been no more phone calls, no mail, no fire in a small trash can on her porch.

What if he arranged for regular patrol drive-bys and went home himself? Or at least let Melinda and the two deputies that had been helping out off the hook?

Maybe—but he knew he'd continue staying here

at night. For a lot of reasons. And, yeah, he'd just gotten into her bed, and he wanted to get back in it.

What kind of bastard did that make him?

Disturbed, he eased out of bed now, picked up his briefs and slipped out of the room. A few minutes later, dressed and pouring his first cup of coffee, he opened his laptop and found several emails from Detective Nakamoto with attachments.

Sipping the coffee, he became absorbed in studying photos and reading what little trace evidence the CSI had found. What Nakamoto hadn't mentioned last night was the fire, this time in a wicker wastebasket. It had burned through but hadn't spread because the flooring beneath it was a laminate that seemed to be impervious to flames. The caption for that photo was, Tell me this means something to you.

Daniel wished it did. All he could do was respond, There's a similar fire at every murder scene. Don't know what it means yet.

He forwarded the information to Boyd and Melinda, then texted them to suggest that the three of them get together today. He asked Boyd if he'd mind driving into town. Daniel wasn't surprised to have Boyd respond within minutes; as a rancher, he was likely up with the sun no matter what. Given that he was now holding down two jobs, he especially had to take advantage of every daylight hour.

Eleven work? he had texted.

Daniel responded as quickly. Let's plan on it.

Frowning, he tried to remember who he'd lined up to stay with Lindsay today. It was getting tougher to find anyone as the days passed without any overt threat. So far, it had been all volunteer. The department was stretched too thin to make paid protection feasible. He'd requested it anyway and been turned down.

He cocked his head at the sound of the shower running just as Melinda called.

"Has Chaney done a single useful thing on this investigation yet?"

Daniel's temper flickered. "I suggested the meeting so that we can try to figure out what we can do that we haven't already done. He may have a fresh perspective."

"What are the odds?" she muttered, but then said, "Sure. Eleven is good for me."

"You might show up with a better attitude," Daniel suggested.

She was quiet long enough he'd have thought she had cut him off except that he could hear her breathing.

"You're right," she said at last. "Chaney rubs me the wrong way, but I can be professional."

The shower went off. Picturing Lindsay stepping out of the bathroom wearing nothing but a towel, he fought to stay focused. "You want to talk about it?"

"No."

Truthfully, that was a relief. His guess was that Boyd and Melinda had gotten personally involved but it hadn't worked out. He'd felt obliged to offer to be a sounding board, but he didn't actually want to know what happened between them.

"Check your email. There was another murder last night," he said. At her exclamation, he gave her the basics, then said goodbye just as Lindsay appeared in the kitchen, looking shy.

Daniel rose to his feet and greeted her with a kiss that he managed to keep gentle. Much as he'd like to go back to bed with her, he didn't have time. Catching this piece of scum had to be his priority.

Lindsay scrambled eggs while he toasted and buttered blueberry bagels. They sat down with their plates and looked at each other.

"When will he stop?" she asked.

Daniel had to shake his head. "I doubt he will. He's killing with scarcely a pause between victims. That's unusual. That he's acting so hastily makes it more likely he'll screw up, but it also has us stumbling behind without time to thoroughly investigate each individual murder the way we normally would."

Poking at her eggs with her fork, Lindsay frowned. "I know you suspect my coworkers, but given that they were working full time, could any of them really pull off this kind of crime spree?"

"It's barely possible," he said. But not likely. He'd been eliminating one after another while cross-referencing their schedules with the likely times of the murders. Increasingly, he agreed with Melinda that they should be looking at ex-employees, not current ones, who had somehow figured out how to get into the database. He'd verified that no ex-employee still had access. That didn't mean they couldn't have an in: either a current employee who sympathized or just liked to complain about all the scumbags who'd gotten off.

Alternatively, a now-retired employee whose rage had been building might have kept a list, dating back years. Who Deserves to Die. That was a realistic possibility...except that the killer had started with two men who had barely gotten into the system. Those identities could only have come by word of mouth.

He was a little surprised at how high the turnover had been in the office. The list of former employees who'd quit or retired in the last three years was keeping him busy. He needed to locate each, find out what they were doing now, run background checks, get some idea of personality and levels of anger. He hadn't attempted to go any further back, because there was one thing Daniel could be sure about: the murderer knew Lindsay.

He surfaced from his brooding when she rose from her chair and said she'd clean. "You're busy, I'm not," she said.

Daniel hid his wince. In her shoes, he'd have been pacing like a tiger testing the bars of his cage, unable to resign himself to inaction. Lindsay hadn't complained recently, but she had to be bored as well as frustrated. She might need a vacation, but home confinement hardly qualified.

Since he needed to get going, he found the protection schedule he'd worked up on his laptop. Theoretically, Phil Chavez, a forty-year-old sergeant on the patrol side, ought to be here any minute. His wife was out of town, leaving him free to spend his day off with Lindsay. He'd encountered her on the job in the past.

Daniel was already reaching for his phone when it rang. Chavez's name came up.

Instead of apologizing because he was running late, the sergeant growled, "I can't make it. I tripped over my own damn slipper and fell. Threw out my back. I can hardly crawl. I had to call Cecelia and ask her to come home."

Daniel told him not to worry, made sure the wife would be home in time to get him to the doctor, and wished him well. He told Lindsay that Chavez couldn't make it and why before he went back to the schedule to see who he could substitute.

Frowning at the monitor, he said, "Maybe you should just come with me. The police station is a fortress." That wasn't literally true, but close enough; it was built with brick, and getting in past the lobby took electronic gymnastics.

She wrinkled her nose. "I think we've gone overboard. Why can't I stay home? Is he really going to break into my house in broad daylight?"

"Most of your neighbors will be at work," he pointed out. "That leaves you isolated."

Those blue eyes fastened beseechingly on him. "I swear, cross my heart, I'll lock up, keep my phone close, call 9-1-1 if I hear anything out of the ordinary. I'm not totally defenseless, you know."

He had to remind himself that in her job, she walked into ugly situations as often as any first responder. That took guts and an ability to ease tensions.

"Do you have a gun?" he asked.

She blinked. "No! But if I hear the back window break, I'll dash out the front and run."

Resigning himself, he said sternly, "While calling 9-1-1 *and* me."

Lindsay rolled her eyes. "Yes, Detective."

He kissed her, said, "Be smart," and left, taking half a dozen looks in his rearview mirror before he lost sight of her small rambler.

SILENCE SETTLED WITH Daniel gone. Lindsay talked herself out of her ridiculous state of unease. It wasn't as if she hadn't spent much of her life alone. Anyway, she heard a neighbor's garage door rising and then descending, traffic on the street in front. People going about their usual business.

Too bad she couldn't.

What she could do was linger over another cup of coffee and the morning newspaper, do some laundry, then read a good book that wasn't true crime or a mystery. At least she didn't have to make forced conversation with near-strangers who had felt compelled to take a shift protecting her.

During those years in foster care, she'd hated knowing how dependent she was on other people—and the necessity of being grateful to them. She hadn't even realized as her stress level rose the past week that it was in part because she'd been thrown back to those old emotions.

Evenings with Daniel here had been…different. Her feelings for him were complicated. He'd passed the point of being a near-stranger, that was for sure, or last night wouldn't have happened. Even so, she wasn't assuming that having sex with her meant that much to him.

With an effort, she kept her attention on her book until lunchtime. Not all that hungry, she still made a salad and ate most of it. The afternoon opened ahead like a stretch of the Sahara. What did she usually do on her days off? she asked herself desperately.

She did errands. Grocery shopped, stopped by the pharmacy and the library—in fact, she had several books that were now overdue. All activities forbidden to her.

Lindsay glanced at her closed laptop. Really, she'd worked. Work was her life.

Had been.

Something had shifted in her. She wasn't sure she wanted to go back to her former life.

She could make lists. She was good at that. Pros and cons of staying with CPS. Potential alternate jobs. Some goals. What did she want out of life?

Right now, a nap sounded really good. Unfortunately, Daniel had been right; in some ways, she was isolated. She had a suspicion napping wouldn't fall under his "be smart" directive.

Okay, she'd finish her book, then maybe do some baking. She didn't have any better ideas, short of painting the kitchen, but that would require her to go out and buy paint.

Settled cozily on the sofa, she opened the book again. Twice in the next hour she caught herself starting to nod off. No surprise—she hadn't gotten very much sleep last night, after all.

After pouring herself a glass of iced tea, Lindsay went back to reading and to fighting off the sleepiness.

The next thing she knew, she jerked, and realized she'd lost the battle, but something had tugged her awake. What...? Her nostrils flared. Was that smoke she smelled? And...did her eyes burn a little?

The sudden, earsplitting screech brought her to her feet. Her heart thudded. Fire alarm. Oh, God, it *was* smoke stinging her nostrils. And...gasoline?

She took a tentative step toward the hall and reared back when she saw flames licking up one wall. She had to get out of the house. Now.

Except, would somebody be waiting for her out there?

Chapter Eleven

Lindsay snatched up her purse and her laptop, looked around hopelessly at everything she couldn't take the time to try to save and raced for the front door. Her hand on the doorknob, she hesitated.

With the fire consuming the back of the house, the arsonist would expect her to exit out the front. Heart racing in fear, she edged over to the picture window and cracked the blinds. Nobody was visible in the slice of the porch and lawn she could see…but that didn't mean somebody wasn't there. Waiting for her.

She turned as thick, oily smoke billowed into the living room. It smelled terrible. Taking a deep breath, she willed herself to hold it as she desperately scanned the house for options. Her gaze locked on the dining room window. She could get that one open.

Of course she had to pull up the blinds before she could wrench the sash upward. She didn't see anybody waiting outside here, either, but belatedly realized that the old wood-framed window didn't exactly glide upward. A man hidden just out of sight would hear it.

She was out of time.

The air escaped her lungs in a rush. In exchange, she sucked in smoky air. In seconds she began to cough. Eyes watering, she shoved the screen outward. Hungry for fresh air, she tossed her purse and laptop onto the lawn, then swung a leg over the sill and lowered herself gingerly to one side of the thorny old rose bush. Falling to her knees, she couldn't stop coughing.

Movement out of the corner of her eye brought her head up—but she heard multiple sirens, too.

Lights flashing and siren screaming, Daniel drove like a madman. He wouldn't get there soon enough, but he had to try. Firefighters and a patrol officer would have been dispatched and were sure to beat him to Lindsay's house. He hoped like hell they would. The idea of her terrified as she tried to hide behind a neighbor's garden shed or crouch in shrubbery scared him so much his foot pushed down hard on the gas pedal even though the light ahead of him had just turned yellow.

The column of black smoke rose to the sky like a beacon. Midsummer like this, even the grass and foliage would be bone-dry. This time of year, the fire department would be on high alert, but the color of this smoke was a dead giveaway. Gasoline or another accelerant had been used to start the fire.

Arson, and not just the kind of small blaze a troubled kid might start in a wastebasket.

EXACTLY FOUR MINUTES LATER, Daniel turned onto Lindsay's block, where a red fire truck initially blocked his view of her house. Arcs of water criss-crossed to meet the flames as firefighters dragged hoses around the small rambler. Half of them were turned on the walls and roofs of neighboring houses, an acknowledgement that her place was a goner.

He parked behind a squad car and jogged forward, searching frantically for Lindsay in the small crowd that had gathered. Though he desperately needed to find her, at his first full sight of her house he had to stare for a moment. Despite the water combating the fire, voracious flames still shot upward. It was hard to hear anything but the crackling of those angry flames and the splintering sounds as walls and trusses gave way.

Sickened, he resumed his search for her. She'd just lost everything. What Daniel cared about right now was that help had arrived in time to save her. If so… where was she? He'd made plain that she was the priority over the fire. He couldn't believe—

At that moment, he spotted the ambulance. Relief felt like a blow to the chest. He stopped dead where he was on the sidewalk, unaware of the action around him, focused utterly on her. Lindsay sat in the open back, her stricken gaze fixed on the destruction of her home. She couldn't have had time to rescue much of anything before she got out. For a fleeting moment, Daniel tried to imagine how he'd feel, knowing everything he owned was gone: photos and keepsakes from his parents and past relationships, the dining room table he'd spent hours restoring and the oak floors in his home that he'd sanded and stained himself. His favorite riding boots, his leather jacket, the ceramic bowl from a local artisan he used for mixing pancakes.

Once in a new home, Lindsay might spend years reaching for something that had burned to ashes long ago. In her case, she didn't seem to have any family. Anything she'd had to remind her of her parents or grandparents was gone unless she'd stored it in a safe deposit box at the bank. At last he started walking again. She looked worse the closer he got. It had to be shock that had bleached her so pale. A black smear ran from one cheekbone down over her chin. A thick bandage wrapped an upper arm. She held her hands, closed into fists, pressed against her belly. No tear tracks on her cheeks, though. Would she let herself cry later?

As he watched, she began to cough harshly.

Ten feet away, he said her name. He doubted she could hear him, but her head turned and she saw him. She quit hacking and didn't so much as blink. He didn't think he did, either, as he closed the distance.

Either she launched herself into his arms or he snatched her up, he didn't know, only that he held her tight. He lost awareness of their surroundings, the hose snaking inches from his feet, raised voices, even the heat.

"Damn, Lindsay," he murmured, his mouth by her ear. "You're all right. I've been so afraid—" He broke off, as much because his throat closed as because he didn't want to admit that he'd never been scared for another person the way he had been for her.

"I didn't hear a thing," she mumbled. "Somebody set this, didn't they?"

"Oh, yeah," he said grimly.

"The first thing I knew, there was the smoke and then my alarm. I was reading and…" She sounded ashamed. "I think I'd nodded off. I didn't get very much sleep last night. Um. I guess you know that."

He was to blame for her lack of sleep. He didn't want to think about how he'd have felt if she'd died in this fire.

"How'd you get out?" he asked.

"The dining room window."

"Did you see anybody?"

She went utterly still, as though she'd quit breathing. Then, so quietly he could barely hear her, she said, "I think somebody was right around the corner of the house. I saw movement, but then sirens blasted close enough, it must have scared him away."

His grip tightened. "I'm sorry about this. So damn sorry. If I'd had somebody here today—"

"He might have set the fire anyway."

She was right, but he still doubted it was coincidence that the fire was set the first time she'd been left alone since the phone call.

He felt her draw a deep breath, after which she started hacking again. An EMT he recognized helped her back to her seat in the ambulance and covered her face with an oxygen mask.

Daniel promised to come back as soon as he talked to several people.

The fire chief grimaced when Daniel tracked him down. "I'll be surprised if the accelerant isn't good, old-fashioned gasoline. Smell kind of hits you as soon as you get here."

"I noticed," Daniel said. "Damn, I wish we could get our hands on this guy."

"Detective McIntosh just got here. She seems to think this fire is connected to one of your investigations."

"There's no doubt. Especially..." He hesitated, not wanting to put any ideas in Chief Randolph's head. "You notice anything unusual?"

"One of the firefighters mentioned something odd. It's around back, near the point of origin."

Daniel followed him, the two circling onto the street and around the house on the corner to avoid the activity. Fortunately, neither backyard was fenced in. Both stopped when the roof of her house collapsed with a deep groan, but the water seemed finally to be knocking back the fire, albeit too late. Soaking the neighboring houses looked like it had saved them from dangerous sparks.

This wasn't a wastebasket, Daniel saw immediately. Instead, a full-size metal barrel, blackened by the fire, had been placed in the middle of her lawn. The barrel was full of water now because of the hoses, but charred bits of something unidentifiable bobbed on the surface.

"My firefighter says there was a fire in it when he

first came around back." Watching Daniel, Randolph lifted his eyebrows. "You don't look surprised."

"I'm not." Although, damn, he didn't like the escalation implied by a large metal barrel versus wastebaskets. "I'd appreciate it if you and anyone else who saw this keep it to yourselves."

"No problem." The chief's gaze touched on the barrel, then swept the still smoldering ruins of Lindsay's small rambler. "Your guy really likes fires."

"So it seems."

"A BARREL?" LINDSAY REPEATED. "Metal?" It was hours later; she'd finally been turned loose from the ER and was beside Daniel in his truck, on the way to his house. He had been telling her what little he'd learned thus far. "Where did he get one?"

"They're readily available. The recycling place used to sell them, although I don't know if they still do. I have a burn barrel myself," he said tersely. "In rural areas, a lot of people do."

Clutching the seat belt with both hands, she gazed ahead through the windshield as a troubling memory stirred without quite taking form. What was it she remembered about a fire in a barrel? Was this from college? Or one of her foster homes? She suddenly recalled one of her foster fathers burning trash in an ugly, rusting barrel back behind their house. It always stank, and the smoke was an awful color, but they'd lived on acreage, so there was no one near enough to be bothered.

But that wasn't the memory that niggled at her.

It refused to surface, however, either because of her headache or because it was something she'd heard about secondhand.

Finally defeated, she shook her head.

"You know something," Daniel said.

"No, just…" She lifted one shoulder. "I feel like I heard something, but I can't remember what."

"Hmm." He put on the turn signal, his ranch road ahead on the right. "It'll come to you."

He sounded tense, and she understood why. He probably wanted to turn her upside down and shake her until the memory fluttered loose. This was important. Somebody else might die any time.

She shuddered. Who was she kidding? *She* could have died today. If she'd really fallen asleep, she might have been overcome by smoke and never awakened at all. She'd read somewhere that most fatalities in home fires succumbed to smoke long before the flames reached them.

Her dismal mood retreated somewhat when Daniel's converted barn home came in sight. The work and imagination that had gone into it was part of what captivated her.

Between one blink and the next, she had a vision so real, fear gripped her. Flames roared out of the loft, climbing toward the roof, intent only on devouring the structure. The reclaimed wood floors and walls had to be dry. There was no hope—

She blinked again, and there was no fire. Of course there wasn't.

Even so, that fear metamorphosed into panic. She

cried, "Stop! You shouldn't have brought me here. I should go somewhere else."

"What?" Daniel didn't brake.

"He could be following us, or guess this is where I'd have gone." Her voice rose with urgency. "He'll burn down your house, too. You know he will."

"Over my dead body," he said grimly.

"Daniel, please!" She was horribly afraid those were tears stinging her eyes.

Instead of parking in front, he backed into a structure with weathered board siding that she only now realized was a detached garage with a concrete floor and a door that ran on rails overhead. He still held the remote in one hand.

Daniel turned off the engine and, instead of getting out, looked at her. "Nobody followed us. I kept an eye out. And why would this guy assume I'd have brought you home?"

"Because we're—" Wait. Nobody else would have any way of knowing they had slept together. People at CPS probably thought their relationship was still antagonistic. It wasn't as if they'd dined out or gone dancing. "He must have been watching the house," she said more slowly. "He knows you've spent every night there."

Gaze unwavering, he said, "I'd have done the same even if we weren't involved."

He'd guessed what she had almost said. "When you got to the fire tonight, you…you came straight to me. You held me."

He didn't say anything for a minute. She couldn't

imagine that he comforted every distraught woman the same way in the course of his job.

"It's unlikely he was close enough to see us. The place was swarming with cops and firefighters."

"What if he *is* a cop?" she asked. "We've been assuming he'd gotten into the CPS database, but the police were involved in the investigations of all the murder victims. If he's in law enforcement, he wouldn't *need* our records."

Suddenly, she couldn't read Daniel's face.

THE SAME WORRY had struck him, but Daniel had so far pushed back at it. Now, he had to ask himself whether he just hadn't wanted to admit a possibility that was so close to home.

The silence stretched. He had to break it.

"The thought has occurred to me," he admitted. "There are a few problems with it, though. Some of those investigations weren't Sadler PD, they were sheriff's department. We talk but don't share full access to records." Lindsay opened her mouth, but he held up his hand. "Second, no one officer has been involved with even two of those cases. Neither we nor the county have an officer who specializes in child abuse investigations."

"Maybe he didn't investigate any of those cases. He just heard about them, and it rankled. If he'd been abused as a child, and authorities had failed him—"

He cut to the chase. "Then why the obsession with *you*? Why did he believe you'd 'understand'? Do you have cops as friends? Anyone you've worked with enough, he might think he knows you?"

Lindsay shook her head. Twice.

Daniel narrowed his eyes. "Do you have any friends who were abused as children? Maybe you exchanged stories?"

"No," she whispered. "I mean, there are a few foster parents locally who have that kind of background, but I only know that secondhand. I don't deal directly with foster parents, except those who take only emergency placements."

He opened his mouth, then shut it. No, he couldn't ask if she had any friends at all. That would be cruel, and he had a suspicion that the answer would be no. She undoubtedly had women she considered friends, the kind she might meet for a movie, say, but that wasn't the same as close friends who knew you through and through, flaws and all, who'd be there for you in any crisis and knew you'd rush to their aid, too. Lindsay, he thought, had learned to be solitary a long time ago and still maintained the emotional distance that had saved her as a child from the crash when hope and trust were betrayed.

Alarmed by the sudden certainty that he wanted to be the person she could trust, he only nodded and got out of the pickup. Clutching two bulging shopping bags, Lindsay followed suit and met him at the back bumper.

"I hope the stuff fits," he said, feeling awkward. Melinda had offered to pick up a few necessities for a woman who now owned absolutely nothing that hadn't been in her handbag or laptop case. He hoped she'd taken into account the fact that Lindsay's figure was curvier than hers.

He kept a sharp eye on their surroundings as they crossed the short distance to a side door that let directly into his kitchen. No movement caught his eye, except for the horses that grazed nearby, unconcerned.

The usual sense of peace enveloped him inside the house once he closed and locked the door behind them. High windows filled the kitchen with light. The well-used wood for cabinets, walls and floors gave him a sense of continuity, the knowledge that the past was all around.

Looking at Lindsay's dirty, strained face, he said gently, "The house has sprinklers. Using all reclaimed wood the way I did, it seemed prudent."

She stared at him as if she didn't quite understand what he was saying.

"I'm going to put you up in the loft. If you'd prefer, I can sleep down here." He put a hand on her back and steered her toward the stairs.

In the end, he found scissors for her to cut tags off the new clothes and left her alone to take a shower while he started dinner.

As he sliced chicken breasts, he brooded about the deadly intent behind today's assault on her. That was what it was. The fire was attempted murder, not meant only as a warning or to scare Lindsay. He grudgingly supposed it was possible the killer assumed that since it was daytime she would be awake and would flee the house sooner. But once the fire gathered strength and she hadn't appeared, he could have called her or made a noise to draw her attention. Instead, whoever the SOB was, he'd stood back and waited with a spider's patience for her to come to him—if she made it out of the house at all.

Filled with angry tension, Daniel realized he'd sliced the chicken into slivers instead of the thicker pieces he'd intended, but maybe this was a task made for his mood. He grabbed a bell pepper and started in on it.

Whack. Whack. Whack.

By the time Lindsay showed up, he had himself under better control. The stir-fry came perilously close to being a puree, but she didn't seem to notice. He had to keep reminding her to eat.

"I should have called my insurance agent today," she said out of the blue.

"Tomorrow is soon enough."

Her gaze finally met his. "I don't suppose I can look for a new place to live, or go shopping, or…"

He shook his head. He didn't want her appearing anywhere the wrong person might see her. Now that she wasn't even surrounded by her own stuff, her own space, she'd feel imprisoned even more, but he couldn't think of another solution.

Except that cruise. Too bad he'd discovered how much he'd hate not knowing where she was every minute of the day, not being able to talk to her when he needed to. Not being able to see her would leave a huge hole that he feared had nothing to do with the threat to her.

Didn't it figure, that was the moment where she burst out, "You were right. I shouldn't have stayed in town. I'm a burden, not a help! I don't even know what I thought I could do. If I'd put the pieces together, I could have called you from Alaska or the Caribbean or wherever I'd gone." She pressed her lips together, then said, more quietly, "It's not too late for me to go. After dinner, I'll—"

"No," he heard himself say. "I need to be able to ask you questions. Bounce ideas off you." Was he being selfish? Daniel didn't know. "Have you where I can see you."

She stared at him in shock, and he thought she'd heard more than he'd said. Seeing beneath the surface—she was good at that.

Chapter Twelve

"Do you have to sleep downstairs?" Lindsay hovered on the second step leading to the loft. She knew she sounded anxious. Well, so what. She didn't think she could sleep in Daniel's big bed with no idea where he was or what he was doing. What if somebody slipped by him? The staircase was so solid, she wouldn't hear even a single step squeak a warning.

"That's up to you." He regarded her from those dark eyes. "I'd rather sleep with you."

"Please," she said shakily. Right this minute, she needed him as she'd never needed anyone.

He turned out lights and followed her. She was already under the covers when he set down his phone on the bedside table followed by something that landed with a clunk. His big, black pistol. Maybe that should disturb her, but instead it reassured her. He disappeared into the bathroom, emerging with his chest bare above a low-slung pair of flannel pajama pants. She couldn't look away, but he gave her a crooked smile as he lifted the covers and joined her in bed.

"Don't tempt me," he said in a low, growly voice.

"I wasn't injured."

"Walking upstairs was enough to set you off coughing." He reached out a long arm and turned off the bedside lamp, then drew her into his arms, carefully arranging her half sprawled on him, her head on his shoulder.

The tenderness in his touch made her eyes sting. Lindsay shifted her hand until she could feel the slow beat of his heart beneath her palm.

She dropped off to sleep with astonishing speed.

WHEN SHE AWAKENED with a jolt, she discovered she was alone in bed. Sitting up, clutching the sheet to her chest, she battled panic. Where was Daniel? He would have told her if he had to leave, wouldn't he?

Then it registered that sunshine flooded the loft through the skylight. Oh. It was morning. In fact, when she spotted the clock, the display said 8:55.

Lindsay hustled to take a brief shower and get dressed in a pair of crisp new jeans that fit surprisingly well and a pale russet, V-necked T-shirt. Melinda had even provided a hairbrush and elastics. Feet in new flip-flops, Lindsay took a last look at herself in the mirror, amazed at how good she felt. Apparently ten uninterrupted hours of sleep worked miracles. Despite everything, she was smiling as she went downstairs.

Daniel stood by the kitchen table, looking down at a newspaper. His jaw was clenched so hard, she expected to hear molars cracking.

"What's wrong?"

He glanced up, clearly angry. "Somebody has a big mouth. A reporter found out about the trash can fires."

"Oh, no." That was the one detail police had determined to withhold. "But...who?"

"God knows."

She frowned, sitting down and turning the front page so she could read the article, too. Last night, there'd been more witnesses than usual, but the smaller fire had not only been in back, it had been set in the barrel. To anyone who didn't know better, it would look as if flying embers from the house had blackened the metal.

Daniel controlled himself well enough to pour her a cup of coffee and ask if scrambled eggs and toast were okay.

She'd done most of the cooking when he'd stayed at her house, so she only nodded.

His back to her as he cracked eggs, he said, "I told the fire chief about the previous fires. I asked him to keep it to himself. I can't believe he'd turn around and spout off to a reporter immediately."

She'd spoken to the man, too, and he'd been really kind. "It had to be somebody else. I mean, how many crime scene investigators and cops have seen them? If one of them told a friend, or a couple of them were overheard talking about it..."

"I'll see their asses fired if I find out who gave out this information," he snapped.

She kept quiet for a minute as he dumped the

beaten eggs into a hot pan. Finally, she asked, "Does it really matter?"

He huffed out a breath. "I don't know. Maybe we'll get lucky now and someone will step forward and say, 'I knew this guy who liked to start fires in wastebaskets at school, and even sometimes as a joke when he was at friends' houses. I wonder…'"

"That's possible."

He grabbed thick slabs of toast as they popped up from the toaster and slapped on butter. "You're more optimistic than I am."

Lindsay blinked at that. "I don't think anyone has ever called me an optimist."

The smile that creased Daniel's cheeks was a big improvement on his previous grim expression. "There's always a first time."

She examined how she felt, expecting devastation because of everything she'd lost yesterday. But Daniel gave her a sense of hope. Maybe deep inside she *had* been nurturing a sense of optimism. Who knew she could?

DANIEL SIPPED COFFEE and watched as Lindsay checked messages on her phone. There were obviously a bunch, and he was intrigued by her ever shifting expressions. Wrinkled nose, surprise, annoyance, quirky smile.

When she reached the end, she said, "How bad news does fly. Twenty-six messages, seven of them from eager reporters."

Curious, he asked, "The others from friends?"

"Mostly. Well, and people I work with. Celeste and Sadie both left messages asking if there was anything they could do."

Celeste, if he wasn't mistaken, was the front desk receptionist.

"Melinda, wondering if the clothes fit right. She said to let her know what else I need. Glenn saying how shocked he was when he saw my house burning on the five o'clock news. He and several other co-workers want me to let them know how I am."

Daniel nodded. That was expected.

Her crinkled forehead and hesitation sharpened his attention.

"Ray Hammond left a message, too. He said he has a spare room if I need someplace to stay."

Daniel snorted. "Spare room, hell. That's not what he has in mind."

"He can't possibly imagine I'd leap into bed with him out of gratitude," she said indignantly. "Although it does seem strange. We're polite, and that's about it. So why would he think…?"

"That you'd be desperate enough to take him up on his offer?" He mulled the question over. "You're right. That is strange."

"Sadie offered me a place to stay, too. She and her husband have a big ranch, pretty isolated. It might not be a bad idea."

He shook his head. "Not happening. Sheriff Chaney offered, too, but someone got out there and murdered the Haycrofts without a soul on the ranch seeing a stranger coming or going."

"But you can't stay with me constantly," she argued.

"No." Frustration roughened his voice. "Today, I think I'll take you with me until I can get a new roster of bodyguards arranged. Worse comes to worst, you can sit in the break room at the station, eat vending machine snacks and read a good book."

She looked as thrilled as she had the last time he'd outlined the same proposal. "Am I safe there if the killer is a cop?" she asked dubiously.

"I don't think he'll turn out to be in law enforcement. No matter what, the station is a busy place in the daytime."

He couldn't blame her for her dubious expression. And she didn't know yet how bare-bones the break room was, or that the only available chairs were designed for a quick sit while you ate your lunch, not a six- or eight-hour stint.

He reminded himself there weren't a lot of choices here.

When he grilled her about how she felt, she claimed to be fine and insisted that she hadn't coughed yet this morning.

He told her she should bring a sweatshirt or sweater since the police station was air-conditioned. Lindsay disappeared upstairs. When she returned, she'd put on socks and bright white athletic shoes and carried an Oregon State University Beavers sweatshirt. Daniel seemed to recall that Melinda had graduated from OSU.

During the short drive into town, he and Lindsay discussed calls she needed to make and what she should and shouldn't tell her friends. Where she was staying topped the "shouldn't" list.

He'd just pulled into the parking lot behind the police station when her phone rang.

"Gayle," Lindsay murmured. She answered, said, "Thank you for calling," then listened with only an occasional interjected word. "Really?"

Gayle was the older caseworker in Lindsay's office. Daniel hadn't gotten a read on her.

He turned off the engine but made no move to get out. He did shift his gaze from mirror to mirror and the windshield, watching for movement. The parking lot might be reasonably safe, but he still felt exposed. He'd have hustled Lindsay into the station, midconversation or not, but he could tell this was no idle chat.

Finally, Lindsay thanked her and said, "I can't believe I've never heard about this before. I really appreciate you telling me."

A moment later, phone still clutched in her hand, she turned in the seat to face Daniel. "Gayle has been with the local office of CPS for, oh, eight or nine years, with an intermission of a couple of years when she couldn't work for health reasons." She took a deep breath. "She says in her early years here, when anyone was especially angry or frustrated, they'd be encouraged to start a fire in a burn barrel out back. Glenn thought it was a healthy outlet. He'd say, 'Every time you're ready to lose it, start a fire.'"

Daniel swore. Way to go for a supervisor: tell his people to start fires to express their rage.

Lindsay bit her lip, then continued, "They had celebrations, too, when a particularly vicious abuser was convicted in court. They'd, um, do things like roast hot dogs or make s'mores. She said it was usually lunch hour, so nobody got drunk or danced naked around the fire, but…"

But overt celebrations couldn't be PC—and Gayle had just tied those small fires firmly to the local CPS.

"Did she say whose idea it was?" he asked.

"Glenn at least condoned it." Lindsay sounded reluctant to say even that much. Now she took a deep breath and met his eyes, her own turbulent. "She also said there'd been a series of fires set in wastebaskets in our offices. Gayle thinks that's why Glenn allowed the burn barrel thing. Eventually, word got out and he was ordered to stop it and get rid of the barrel."

"The surprise is that they got away with something that insane for more than a day," he growled.

Lindsay only nodded.

"Damn." He'd quit paying attention to the people coming and going in the parking lot. "We need to get inside. Wait for me to come around."

Compliance wasn't in her nature, but she didn't argue. The way he hustled her the short distance to the back door probably scared her, but it beat the alternative.

THE DAY WAS incredibly tedious, lanced with occasional anxiety when someone wandering into the break room seemed especially interested in her.

Of course Lindsay knew a number of the officers.

Joe Capek sat down to keep her company for a few minutes and commiserate about her house fire before he went out on patrol. Evidently he'd crossed paths with Daniel, who told him that she was condemned to near-solitary confinement here—or, as he put it, hanging out.

Otherwise, the first stranger in uniform she met was a man who had to be near retirement age. He was barely inside the door when he saw her and came to a halt.

"Who are you and what are you doing here?"

Taken aback not by his question, but rather by his near hostility, Lindsay said, "Detective Deperro brought me here for the day as a safety measure."

"Yours the house that burned down yesterday?"

She nodded.

Finally moving on into the room, he said, "So you're the CPS worker."

"I am."

He grunted, grabbed a plastic dish from the refrigerator and heated it in the microwave, his back to her. When the microwave beeped, he took his meal and left the break room without another word.

"Nice," she mumbled.

An interminable hour later, a tall thin officer around forty entered, his gaze going right to her. "You must be Lindsay Engle."

"I am.".

"Heard you got fired."

She stiffened. "I was suspended with pay only until Detective Deperro arrests the killer."

The cop watched her with enough intensity to have her nerves prickling, especially since he didn't pour himself coffee, go to the refrigerator or drop coins in either of the vending machines. She had the uneasy feeling he was here for the sole purpose of getting a good look at her.

"You can't possibly be mourning any of the scumbags who've died," he said.

Her tension ratcheted up. "Who've *died*? You think they just tipped over when their hearts inexplicably stopped? Surely you know how brutal these killings have been."

He shrugged. "Pieces of shit we won't have to arrest again."

Lindsay felt sure his attitude was as, if not more, common in law enforcement circles than social services. Frustration was inevitable. Either way she didn't like it. Many of the abusers she dealt with had been abused as children themselves, or their anger control issues had other understandable roots. Some were alcoholics—but stopping drinking wasn't as easy as a lot of people wanted to think. She'd dealt with several men who were recently returned veterans battling PTSD. She had also seen plenty of abusive or negligent parents who did kick their drug habit or their alcoholism, or who got a handle on their personal problems in counseling because they loved their children.

Lindsay did not like Officer… She strained her eyes to read his badge. Jones? James? Something like that.

The door opened behind him and Daniel appeared, taking in the situation with a glance. "You need something in here, Jonas?"

The other cop's lip curled in a sneer even as his flat gaze remained on Lindsay. "Nah." Without another word, he left. The door swung shut behind him.

"Wow. Great guy."

"When I saw him heading this way, I thought I ought to intervene." Daniel pulled out a chair beside her. "How are you holding up?"

"Bored but fine. What's his problem?"

"Lousy attitude. He's had a couple of warnings."

"Are you sure that's all?"

He grimaced. "Yeah."

Annoyed, Lindsay said, "You know, all those online videos you see of a cop slamming a teenage girl to the sidewalk seem surreal, until you meet a charmer like Officer Jonas."

He cocked an eyebrow. "And all of your colleagues are compassionate, dedicated, professional and unfailingly patient with the people they have to investigate?"

She wrinkled her nose at him. "Point made."

As always, his grin warmed her. "I ordered lunch from Sandwiches and Such. Hope you're not picky."

"I'm not."

She had to admit she looked forward to lunch after a morning of doing nothing. She hadn't even returned more than a few of the calls that had filled up her voice mail. She didn't feel like talking to anyone she had to suspect. "Have you called Glenn or Sadie about the burn barrel thing?"

"Glenn. He admitted it was his idea. He really thought it was a stress reducer, but he understood why he had to ditch it." Daniel spoke carefully, as if trying not to let his opinion leak into his voice.

"He wouldn't have known about the connection between these killings and the fires until he watched his morning news," she pointed out, ignoring the obvious.

"I'm not jumping to conclusions about him," Daniel said with equal care. "You have to be aware that he does fit the profile in some ways, though."

Lindsay fired back, "Except that he was an amazingly supportive supervisor who taught me everything I know. I can't believe—"

"Whoa!" Laughing, Daniel held up his hand. "I didn't say I was going to arrest him. The truth is, anyone around when everyone in the office vented their frustration with fire could see it now as a symbol. I'd look harder at caseworkers who were here then but have retired, except—"

"For the fact that the killer must know me. Or *thinks* he does." She'd thought about the symbolism in those fires. "What if he's protesting, in a way, that he's being denied the chance to burn away his frustration?"

Daniel shoved back his chair and stood, lines deepening on his forehead. "He's crazy. He could have gone home and lit a damn fire in his fireplace."

Well, yes, that was true, but...

Daniel didn't give her a chance to argue. "Call

people back. Get a sense of how they felt about the famous CPS bonfires, why don't you?"

Then he was gone, leaving her alone with her phone.

As DANIEL BUCKLED his seat belt, he contemplated the fancy building housing the real estate office. He'd just interviewed Hank Cousins, a guy who'd quit his job with Child Protective Services only ten months ago. That meant he'd worked in the same office with Lindsay for two plus years, yet she hadn't mentioned him. He'd be asking why.

Daniel had run the names of former caseworkers—specifically, the ones who still lived locally—by Sadie Culver and Glenn Wilson. Sadie knew Cousins only by reputation. Sounding tolerant, Glenn had said, "Classic burnout. Last thing he said was that no amount of money could make him keep spending his days talking to people who didn't deserve the space they took on this earth."

Cousins interested Daniel more than other names on his list for two reasons: he'd studied for his real estate license for months without anyone in the office knowing he intended to leave, meaning whatever his level of rage he was capable of restraint—and the very nature of selling real estate meant he was hard to track down during the day.

Daniel's phone rang before he left the parking lot. He recognized the number, not surprised when the fire marshal confirmed that Lindsay's house fire had been started with gasoline.

"From the burn pattern, it's obvious this guy wet down a good part of the back wall of the house with gas, and I wouldn't be surprised if he didn't splash some on the roof. Looks like the homeowner had a woodbox out back, the kind with a plywood lid. That would have given him something to boost himself up on."

"No gas can found, I presume."

The fire marshal thought there had to have been at least two five-gallon cans, which would have been heavy.

"He didn't have far to go if he parked on the side street," Daniel pointed out. "The two houses along with the trees and shrubs would have given him some protection from being seen by a passing car. Besides, I'm guessing this SOB had been watching her place and knew which neighbors were gone daytimes."

The marshal grunted his agreement. "My job is easier when arsonists get fancy. This fire could as well have been set by a teenager. The barrel is the only thing we can call a signature, but it may be relevant only to these murders. I have to wonder if he's set fires before that didn't result in fatalities. Maybe just for fun."

Daniel had thought the same. Quite a few years had separated the burn barrel at the CPS office from this outbreak of murder. As fixated as the killer was on fire, it was hard to imagine he'd gone without all that time.

"You plan to look back for similar fires?"

"Damn straight. If I find any strings to pull, you'll

be the first to know," the fire marshal assured him, and signed off.

Fifteen minutes later, Daniel arrived at the home of another ex-CPS employee who had caught his attention. This one lived on acreage outside the city limits. The multiple, deep potholes in the long dirt driveway didn't seem to encourage visitors.

Daniel parked in front of a log house with a carport extending from one side. It had been converted into a workshop. Ross Zeller had left the security of state employment to carve wood with a chainsaw. In fact, in the shade of the carport, a brawny, bearded man was currently working on a six-foot-high log standing upright. Looked like it might become a leaping salmon. He turned when he saw Daniel getting out of his SUV, letting his chainsaw idle.

Daniel didn't rest his hand on the butt of his weapon, but he kept it close. This was the first time he'd found Zeller at home, but neighbors and his former coworkers described him as a strange man. The postal worker had seen him pacing his acreage yelling at someone who wasn't there. His wife had apparently left him about the same time he'd changed careers. Was that one more thing he could blame on the high-stress job and the abusers who were the reason for his burnout?

Any of several outbuildings on the property could be hiding that stolen white Corolla.

The chainsaw coughed and died. Zeller didn't sound friendly when he said, "What's a cop want with me?"

"If you've heard about the string of murders locally, you know fire is part of them."

The big man waited warily.

"I'm trying to talk to everyone who worked at CPS when the burn barrel was being employed as a stress-reducer."

Zeller snorted. "That was the best idea Mr. Follow-the-Rules ever had. Surprised me, to tell you the truth."

"Anybody seem to especially enjoy the fires?"

"You're kidding, right? We all enjoyed them. Fire awakens something primitive in all of us. You must know that."

Daniel couldn't deny it. Who didn't stare with fascination into the leaping, multicolored flames of a campfire? "Tying them to a rage to kill is a little different," he said, keeping his tone conversational.

Zeller's expression went chillingly flat. "Wouldn't know. If you don't mind, I have work to do."

Daniel had no excuse to push the guy, so he thanked him for his time and retreated to his vehicle.

As he jolted back down the driveway, Daniel saw in his rearview mirror that Ross Zeller hadn't returned to his carving. Instead, he stood unmoving, watching the cop drive way. Daniel wished he had a clue what Zeller was thinking.

Funny thing: self-employed, living alone, Zeller too was next to impossible to eliminate as a suspect by alibi. Who was there to provide him with one?

Chapter Thirteen

Hustling Lindsay out to his truck at the end of the day, Daniel had to wonder how safe she really had felt here at the police station today, stuck having to deal with cops like Al Jonas. There was a good reason he'd asked only a select group of trusted fellow officers to guard Lindsay.

Maybe he should consider taking her out to the sheriff's ranch after all. Chaney had several men working for him who were retired army rangers—his partner, Gabe Decker, and foreman, Leon Cabrera. Daniel had fought at their sides in the gun battle when they'd been surrounded by the forces of a major drug trafficking organization. If one or the other could assume bodyguard duties…

But Decker was now married and stepfather to Chloe, the little girl he'd been protecting back when Daniel encountered them, and Cabrera had a family, too. Daniel wouldn't want to bring trouble down on them. Besides…damn it, Lindsay would be nothing but a job to either of them, while for him—

He shut down on that thought.

He had more confidence in himself. Right now, that's what mattered.

"Daniel?"

At her soft query, he turned his head. Seat belt fastened, she was watching him.

"Is something wrong?"

Yeah, something was wrong. He had started the truck but not put it in gear. Shaking his head, he lied, "No. I need you to get down on the floorboards, though, just until I'm sure we're not being followed."

As she unfastened the seat belt and crouched down, he grimaced. Like most cops, he tried to keep his address unlisted. Didn't mean he couldn't be found. He entered cutting horse competitions and judged and refereed them, too, ensuring that he was well-known among local horse owners. In fact, too many people knew him. Still, cops didn't take witnesses home with them. Lindsay had been careful to stay away from windows. Unless the guy was staking out his place twenty-four-seven and saw Daniel ushering her into the house, why would he suspect she was staying with him?

Daniel had made the decision to be sure Lindsay had a guard when he couldn't be there, but even though he'd have liked someone else to be there nights, too, adding a bunch more vehicles coming and going would be the equivalent of him waving his arms and shouting, *I have something to protect.*

All the time he brooded, his gaze flicked from mirror to windshield to mirror...and to his passenger.

"Okay," he said gruffly. "You can get up now."

She untangled herself and settled in the seat. "That was fun."

He liked her attitude, a cross between humorous and snide. Under pressure, she didn't buckle; she got mad.

Taking advantage of this uninterrupted time together, he asked about both Ross Zeller and Hank Cousins.

"Hank was friendly, almost too talkative. It was kind of annoying when I was trying to concentrate. I guess I wasn't that surprised he quit. He looked for any distraction from his job, you know? Um. Ross Zeller. He was...unsettling. I don't mean violent or anything," she hastened to say, "just weird." Her nose wrinkled. "It seemed like every time I looked up, he was staring at me."

Daniel mentally ticked off one of the boxes on his list.

"The only thing is, other people told me the same thing, so it wasn't just me. And he never came on to me or even suggested coffee. He was married, though I heard he and his wife split right before he quit."

"I was told the same," Daniel said. "Was he good at his job?"

"I...don't really know," Lindsay said hesitantly. "He was...volatile, I guess is the best word. I think Glenn only assigned him low-level abuse accusations."

Serial killers were often categorized as "organized" versus "disorganized." Lindsay was implying he fell on the "disorganized" side—except that from what Daniel had seen and heard, his carvings were fine and sold for substantial amounts. That meant he was disciplined enough to work hard. He'd been cagey when Daniel talked to him, too.

But disciplined in one way didn't mean he could study to commit a series of murders without being seen, without leaving any trace evidence.

Cousins might have that kind of discipline if he was truly dedicated to a goal—but nothing about him had sent up a flare for Daniel.

And then there was Glenn, who still hung around the CPS offices, continued to befriend Lindsay in particular, but offered advice and support to other caseworkers, too. Glenn, Daniel had only recently discovered, had been there the day Lindsay got the call about Shane Ramsey collapsing after his uncle beat him.

Daniel hadn't so much as hinted to Lindsay recently that Glenn was still on his radar. Her affection for the man she called a mentor blinded her where he was concerned. On the other hand, Daniel had gained a lot of respect for her ability to judge people. Glenn might be as great a guy as she thought he was.

Deciding this was a good time to change the subject, he smiled. "Hope you like quesadillas. That's what we're having tonight."

"You mean I don't have to cook?"

He laughed. "Your house, you cooked, my house, I cook."

"Works for me," she said. "Might be a long time before I have to cook again."

The humor didn't quite come off.

He reached for her hand, and she returned his clasp.

"YOU EVER DONE any shooting?"

Daniel's question came out of left field, but she should have expected it.

Spreading pico de gallo atop her black bean quesadilla, she said, "Yes, when I was thirteen... No, maybe fourteen. I wasn't in that home very long. The man was a gun nut, and after the police came out to the house because he'd taken his AK-15 along to issue a threat to a neighbor, we kids got moved."

Daniel offered her sour cream. "Sounds like a winner."

"He freaked us out." She wrinkled her nose. "I swear the guy owned fifty guns or more. He talked about being ready to defend his family when the government came to try to take away his weapons." She paused. "He must not have mentioned them when he was interviewed by social services."

Daniel laughed, although he was watching her more perceptively than she liked. "Another reason behind your career path."

"Maybe. He wasn't abusive, though."

He said something harsh under his breath, and she realized she'd put too much emphasis on the *he*. Yes, she'd been placed in homes where people meant to protect her had hurt her instead. In one home, she'd had to drag her dresser in front of the bedroom door at night to keep the man out. That one had been bad;

she'd just reached puberty and been self-conscious as it was about her developing body. Vulnerable, afraid to speak out, she'd gotten lucky when the foster mom complained to the caseworker about the scratches on the bedroom floor. The caseworker had her pack up and removed her from the home within the hour.

Yet another reason for her life choices, of course.

"Weren't you ever in a home where people were good to you?" he asked, a roughness in his voice.

"Yes, I stayed in the same home my last three years. I still call and occasionally visit my foster parents." She hesitated. "I'm sure they'd take me in now, but—"

She could tell he didn't like the idea, but he said, "But?"

"They always have three or four kids living with them. I couldn't put them at risk."

"I wouldn't let you," he said shortly, and resumed eating.

She did the same. He continued with the questions about her childhood, and she told him more than she'd intended. More than she usually told anyone. If she had caught even a whiff of pity, she'd have shut down, but Daniel's reactions were never what she considered the norm.

They had finished eating and she was clearing the table as he started the coffee when her phone rang. Made instantly wary, she went to grab it from her handbag. Glenn was the caller.

Relaxing, she signaled to Daniel, who nodded, and

she took the phone into the part of the open space situated to form a sort of living room.

"Glenn," she said, as she sank onto a leather sofa, one foot under her. "You calling for an update on the latest exciting turn my life has taken?"

His familiar chuckle was reassuring. "Tough lady."

"What, you thought I'd sit in a corner and suck my thumb?"

Glenn laughed again. "Not for a minute. I just wanted to find out how you're holding up, but I guess I don't have to ask."

"I'm okay. Really."

"I assume you've had plenty of offers for places to stay."

Aware that Daniel had come from the kitchen to lean against a wall where he could hear her, she said, "Yes, I have. Is that why you called?"

He snorted. "You don't want to move in with a crusty old man like me. I hope you know I'd offer if you were desperate, but I'm sure you have younger, more gallant men eager to take you in."

Uneasiness stirred for the first time. Was he angling for her to say, *Sure, you've met Detective Deperro, haven't you? I'm staying with him*.

Instead of too obviously evading her question, she said, "Like Ray Hammond, you mean?"

"You're serious?"

"Yep. I'd have sworn I'm low on his list of favorite caseworkers."

"I knew there was tension between you," he admitted. "He probably means well..."

Somehow, she wasn't surprised that he trailed off midsentence. White lies weren't Glenn's style.

"Well," she said briskly, "I've had so many invitations, I'll probably hop from household to household so I don't wear out my welcome. I do need to start figuring out whether I'm going to rebuild or..." She was the one to break off this time. That was a big *or*. If she didn't plan to go back to her job, maybe she'd be better off moving, starting afresh.

Painfully aware of Daniel's presence, she knew she wouldn't be going anywhere until she found out whether their relationship might become serious.

Seizing her chance, she said, "Detective Deperro told me the burn barrel out behind the office was your idea. Did you really think you'd get by with that?"

He laughed. "Got by with it longer than I expected." His tone sobered. "I never imagined anything like what happened to you. I was trying to manage creatively. We were having trouble retaining caseworkers. You know what it's like. If they could learn to vent, I thought they'd quit repressing the anger and frustration, not throw in the towel so quick."

"That actually makes sense," she admitted.

"I'm glad you understand. You know how highly I think of you."

All she could think to say was "thank you."

To her relief, Glenn didn't press her for her current or future whereabouts, just ended the conversation by saying, "Call if you need to talk."

Off to the side, Daniel said unexpectedly, "It's not

just women who feel scorned when they're rejected, you know."

Lindsay swiveled on the sofa. "What?"

"Ray."

"You think he was, I don't know, trying to apologize or something when he offered me a place to stay?"

"Maybe."

She thought about it. "I was polite when I said no, thanks."

Daniel kept his distance. "Learn anything from your call?"

Lindsay told him about Glenn's rationale and her reaction before hesitating. "There was only one thing."

He lifted his eyebrows.

"When he said 'I'm glad you understand.'"

"'I thought you of all people would understand,'" Daniel quoted.

"Yes." She found herself shaking her head. "I won't believe Glenn would do any of this. Why would he now that he's retired, putting the job behind him?"

Offering no reassurance, Daniel watched her for a minute before pushing away from the wall. "I'm going to have you start carrying my backup handgun. For now, forget Glenn and Hammond both. Let's go upstairs."

To bed, remained unspoken.

"THIS WAS AN ugly one," Daniel said tersely.

Lindsay had pounced on the phone when she saw

his number on the screen, but hearing his news about the latest murder, she quailed. "Who is it?"

Of course she wasn't alone at Daniel's house. Officer Alvarez, today's bodyguard, was currently at the back of the house walking from window to window, watching for anything out of the ordinary. For all she knew, Daniel had already called or texted him about the latest murder.

In answer to her question, Daniel said, "Ryan Olson."

She felt a brief moment of hope that she might not have been the caseworker involved with this victim. "I don't remember that name."

Daniel killed her tentative hope. "You're the caseworker of record. It was... Let me check. Three years ago."

Ryan Olson. Dredging her memories, she still came up short.

"I must have just started working here—" Her heart sank. "Wait. I do remember. I wasn't involved in the investigation. I was handed nominal responsibility for the case because my successor left for a new job. Olson took a plea, so that was that."

"He got a slap on the wrist."

"Well, even though he hurt those two boys pretty bad, it was a one-time event." The details were coming back to her.

"His kids?"

"His son and a friend. They were wild, and he blew his top and burned them both."

Daniel was quiet for a minute. "How?"

"Um…forced their hands down onto the top of the wood stove. He started to push his boy's face down, too, but came back to himself in horror. He tried to treat the burns he'd given them, but didn't take them for medical care."

"Bet that didn't look good."

"No. When his wife got home, she took them. I seem to remember that he was a veteran who came home in bad shape. Couldn't sleep, screamed at his wife and kids. You know. But he hadn't hurt anyone until then, which is why he got away with probation and counseling."

"Did the wife stay with him?"

"I won't swear to it, but I think so." She'd already been wrapped up in other investigations, grateful this one wasn't her problem. "The other family was angry he didn't get time in prison."

"Don't suppose you remember their names?"

"Not a chance." She frowned. "Are you thinking this could be a copycat murder?"

"Crossed my mind." Daniel continued, "He was killed inside the Sadler city limits, which makes me primary. It'll be a while before I can get away. I'll call Alvarez and make sure he can stay."

"I can talk to him—"

Daniel interrupted with a brusque "I'll do it." When he added, "We'll get this piece of crud," he sounded considerably gentler.

If only she could help instead of being a burden.

She heard a ring tone and turned to see Officer Tom Alvarez already putting his phone to his ear.

He watched her with eyes as dark as Daniel's during the brief conversation. His end consisted of "uh-huh" and "sure." When he set down his phone on the tiled countertop beside his perch on a stool, he said, "Another murder?"

Lindsay nodded. "I hardly remembered the victim. Ryan Olson."

He shook his head.

She told him what she remembered, and saw the same puzzlement she felt.

"Unless something worse happened later, he seems like an unlikely victim."

"Very. Plus…the killer has targeted abusers from my caseload. I never even *met* this guy."

"Huh."

Alvarez had been really nice, making an effort to be companionable as well as perform his bodyguard duties. Now he suggested they play poker for paperclips. He talked about his children with pride that made something in Lindsay ache. Of course, he showed her pictures on his phone of his four kids, from a ten-year-old to his oldest, a girl wearing her prom dress.

"She's really beautiful." Lindsay handed him back his phone. "Is that her boyfriend?"

"Not for long." Alvarez flashed her a grin. "She's been accepted at Stanford. The little punk is heading for a community college."

Despite everything churning inside her, Lindsay laughed. "He can't be that bad if she likes him."

"He's okay, but not good enough for my little girl."

"I'll bet he's scared of you, too."

"Of course he is. I carry a gun."

Lindsay knew he was trying to distract her, and she let him think he'd succeeded. Once he made the rounds inside the house, going from window to window, her thoughts reverted immediately to Daniel's call and the grimness and revulsion she'd heard in his voice.

This was an ugly one. She didn't think of herself as a coward, but she wasn't sure she wanted to know any more.

"HE'S LOSING IT," Chaney growled.

Daniel would call that a major understatement. He wasn't alone in having trouble tearing his gaze from the gruesome sight of what had been a big, strong man in his late thirties. For all that Chaney must have seen in war zones, he looked sick. Melinda was hiding her feelings better, probably because she'd developed that to an art form. As a rare woman cop in these parts, she had to appear hard even when she was grieving, horrified or scared.

Daniel let out a long breath. "What if our killer knows the parents of the other boy Olson burned?"

Melinda answered. "Maybe it's just the use of fire—burning the kids—that stuck in his memory."

"Could be this murder gave him a chance play with fire," Chaney muttered.

They all watched in silence as the body bag was zipped up and lifted onto a rolling gurney. Daniel wanted to be relieved, but he wouldn't be forgetting anytime in the near future the sight of what this victim had suffered. The number of burns... He pushed the images away.

Overpowering this victim wouldn't have been easy. Zeller was the suspect who leaped to mind. He had massive arms and spent his days hefting logs and controlling a chainsaw.

What it came down to was that the man who had tortured Ryan Olson was still out there, still furious at Lindsay for failing to appreciate his multiple "gifts." This feeling of helplessness wouldn't have sat well with Daniel at any time, but it was intolerable given his fear for her.

"Not a single witness so far, and I'm betting we don't find one," Daniel said flatly. "He plans. He has to be cold-blooded as hell even with the anger driving him."

"He burns," Melinda observed, her tone strange.

Daniel waited for Chaney to jump on her, but all he did was turn his head to look at her. His expression was odd, too, Daniel thought.

Hell. They were all in a mood. How could they help it? The killer hadn't just escalated; he'd become more vicious than a rabid wolf. Why?

Daniel hadn't realized he'd spoken his thoughts aloud until Melinda answered.

"Because Lindsay escaped. He needed to punish her, and he failed. Maybe this—" she gestured toward where the body had lain "—was a roaring temper tantrum."

The ball of fear knotted even tighter in Daniel's

gut. Had this been a message to Lindsay? Or had this bastard used another man's suffering to make himself feel better? Powerful. In control.

It was maddening to know that a serial killer *was* in control. To think how much pleasure he must be taking as he watched the cops flail around incompetently.

Distantly aware his hand was shaking when he lifted it to rub his jaw, Daniel wanted to walk away from this crime scene. Just get in his car and drive, to hell with speed limits, until he could see and touch Lindsay. And then he wanted not to leave her side until the killer fixated on her was behind bars or dead.

Preferably dead.

It was the first time in his career as a law enforcement officer he'd thought that.

Gaze intense on his face, Melinda said, "Are you sure he doesn't know you took Lindsay home?"

"How can he?"

She lifted her eyebrows. "If he was watching the night her house burned, he saw the way she walked into your arms, how you held her. I wasn't there, but I've heard people talking."

"But even if he hung around long enough to see me drive away with Lindsay, I could have dropped her anywhere." Damn, he wished he didn't share Melinda's unease. Logic was on his side, but the uncanny way the killer had gotten each victim alone, committed his horrors without anyone hearing a sound or catching a glimpse of him coming and going...

"What's the alternative?" he growled, arguing with himself as much as with Melinda. "Anywhere I take her, we could be seen. As it is, I have her covered day and night."

They threw around ideas, but the truth was, there were only so many alternatives. Sending her off on a world cruise would have more appeal if he really believed they'd catch this monster by the time she returned home.

As it was, the killer was playing them.

"We need to keep canvassing," he said abruptly.

Chaney snorted. "We're not going to find him that way. We all know that. He's had hours to vanish." He raised a hand to prevent Daniel's retort. "We have to do it anyway, but why don't you let us handle it?"

Melinda nodded. "Go home, Daniel."

He was primary. He should work this investigation until he was ready to drop. But moved by their unusual unified stance, Daniel said hoarsely, "Thanks."

The urgent need driving him to get back to Lindsay was a little bit of a shocker. Wanting to believe she was safe at his place wasn't the same as being deep-down convinced. Heading for his department-issued vehicle, it was all he could do to keep his pace to a walk.

No, he wasn't going to stop at the station to switch to his pickup. What he did intend to do was go by Ross Zeller's home, see if his strangeness was any more evident. And maybe ask if *he* had a burn barrel.

Chapter Fourteen

Lindsay rocketed out of sleep, for a moment disoriented. What had she heard? She strained for any sound out of the ordinary, but the night was quiet. A bad dream, she decided, her heart still pounding, but she'd woken Daniel, who also sat up.

"What is it?"

"I—probably nothing. A nightmare."

He slid out of bed and went to the French doors, easing the blind to one side. After a minute, he said, "I don't see anything, but I'm going out to walk the perimeter."

Her fingernails bit into her palms. He kept doing this, scaring her every time. "Please don't. What if—" She couldn't finish. He'd know what she hadn't said. *What if he kills you? What if he sees you leaving the house and comes in?*

Already half-dressed, he paused. "I know how to be a ghost."

Shakily, she said, "So does he."

He went still, his shirt half on. "He could be ex-military. I don't know why that hasn't occurred to me."

As far as she could tell, Daniel was energized by the idea and unswayed by her fears.

After yanking down the shirt, he shoved his feet in his boots, grabbed his gun and murmured, "Stay here." Then he was gone.

Discovering she felt trapped up here, Lindsay got dressed, too. If something happened—gunshots fired, Daniel's house burst into flames—she could deal better if she wasn't naked. Then, like him, she peeked through the blinds.

The view was severely limited, but the moon cast a silver light tonight that illuminated open ground leading toward the impenetrable darkness of the woods.

Her heart took an extra beat. Something had *moved* in that darkness.

Her eyes burned as she stared. She flashed back to the day she'd found Martin Ramsey's body and first thought someone was watching her from beneath the trees.

In fact, these past few days she'd kept feeling eyes on her. The hair on her nape would prickle, and she'd whirl around but never actually see anyone. Her imagination was working overtime, but so far she'd failed to squelch it.

Right now, she couldn't stand the suspense. She slipped to the head of the staircase, unsure if the darkness inside allowed her to feel safe…or had the opposite effect. *Don't be a coward*, she told herself, and descended, her bare feet silent on the solid steps.

In the kitchen, she saw the lighted numbers on the microwave. 4:39. She wouldn't be going back to sleep.

Which door had Daniel gone out? Would he have left it unlocked?

She stood still, waiting. Tension rose as she pictured him slipping through the night, unafraid.

Only the faintest whisper of sound told her the kitchen door had opened. She eased backward into the hall, so she couldn't be seen if it wasn't Daniel who'd entered so quietly.

The kitchen light came on, she heard a familiar clunk, like a gun being set down, and then water running in the sink.

Swallowing fear she hated feeling, she said, "Daniel?"

"It's me." He stepped into sight, his dark eyes locking onto her. "Why'd you come down? You could still get some more sleep."

Lindsay hoped her laugh sounded less broken to him than it did to her. "Sure. That's going to happen."

He studied her for a moment. "Okay. I'm making coffee." He didn't move, though, instead holding out a hand.

She took it and let him draw her close. She wrapped both arms tightly around him, gripping the T-shirt he wore in both fists. His strong embrace calmed her, as did the steady beat of his heart beneath her ear. He couldn't have seen anything even slightly alarming or he wouldn't be so relaxed, would he?

Finally she drew a deep breath and straightened, letting her arms drop to her sides. He did the same but never looked away from her.

"This is getting to you," he said in a soft growl.

Denial seemed pointless. "I guess it is. What are we going to do, Daniel? We can't go on like this forever."

He shook his head. "I'm not moving you."

Shock zinged her. "I didn't mean that." Accustomed to solitude, she had been surprised how comfortable it was to live with Daniel. No, not just comfortable; the truth was, she loved their quiet talks, his heat and solidity in bed at night, his gentle touches, his openness with her.

Making love with him.

What she had no idea was whether he was as happy or hankered for his lost privacy and quiet.

"We'll get through this. He'll make a mistake or one of us will have an epiphany that leads us to him. I admit, I don't like feeling outsmarted and outmaneuvered."

"You know it's not that. If you could predict his next choice of victim, it would be different, but how can you?"

"We did once. We *warned* the stupid woman, and he still figured out when she'd be alone, killed her and waltzed away without leaving so much as a flake of skin or strand of hair behind."

"That means he's using gloves and... I don't know." A Tyvek suit?

Something changed on Daniel's face. Of course he wasn't telling her everything. Should she push?

He turned and went back to where he'd been filling the coffeepot. After a moment, however, he said,

"We're speculating that he's shaved his body, at the very least."

Having followed him, she found herself staring at his back.

"His head, too?" she asked.

"Best guess is a hood. Maybe the kind divers wear."

"Oh." Glenn, for one, didn't have much hair on his head to start with, she couldn't help thinking. He did have a hairy chest, though. She knew because when he left the top button of his shirt undone, curly gray hair showed. He would have shaved that if—

Shame curdled in her stomach. She *knew* him. He wasn't capable—but then she remembered their last conversations. She hadn't known he'd ever been married. In fact, his personal life was pretty much a mystery to her. But wasn't that kind of stuff really superficial? He'd demonstrated his caring, his leadership, his determination and kindness day after day on the job. *That* was what counted. Nausea swirled through her. Think how hurt he'd be if he knew that, even for the tiniest moment, she'd considered the possibility that *he* might be the monster torturing and murdering people.

"What are you thinking?" Daniel leaned against the counter and regarded her, his arms crossed.

She shook her head. "He can't pull the hood up until he knows no one will see him."

"That's true." He hesitated, watchful again. "I've eliminated Hammond and Grudin once and for all."

She gaped. "How? When?"

"They were both in the office when your house was set on fire. This time, there's no doubt."

Lindsay discovered she didn't know how to feel about that. She hadn't wanted either man to turn out to be so horrible or to find her judgment was that off. She didn't like either of them, but she'd respected them as coworkers. But at least... Well, circle back to the fact that she didn't like either of them. That gave her a few degrees of distance. Given the certainty that the killer would turn out to be someone she knew—

"I should be glad," she blurted out, before she could censor herself.

Daniel's dark eyes narrowed, but he kept his mouth shut. And why not? He had to know what she was thinking.

The next thing he said was almost irrelevant. "If only I had more manpower."

Reluctantly, she asked, "To do what?"

"Put a tail on suspects."

"Do you have suspects?"

"You know I do."

Her lips parted, but he shook his head before she could ask who.

"You've told me what you know about people. You already have enough to stew about," he said.

Normally she would have argued, but she knew he was right. Since she was jittery despite the ridiculously early hour of the morning, she went to the refrigerator. She might not be hungry yet, but she had to do *something*, and they'd have to eat sooner or later.

Daniel relaxed, so subtly most people wouldn't

have noticed, but she'd already become an expert on reading his body language. He wanted to steer her away from what he was thinking, and for now she'd let him get away with it.

TIREDNESS WAS BECOMING an issue. There was a limit to how long he could go on this way, Daniel knew, working all day, taking more what he thought of as brief combat naps at night than really sleeping. He'd learned his capacity and limitations during his deployments in battle zones. He could pace himself only so long before he had to have a good eight hours of deep, truly sustaining sleep.

Assuming the killer was, or had been, a Child Protective Services employee—and Daniel had little doubt—two men had risen from a more general field of possible suspects to become his favorites. Both male, one retired, one who had quit. Both had displayed possibly aberrant behavior on the job, and now that they'd left it, neither had a schedule that made it possible to pin down alibis with any certainty.

Ross Zeller and Glenn Wilson.

A few others were still in the running, but trailing well behind.

Zeller might have been in the number one position, except that Lindsay didn't sound as if she'd been very close to him. He'd stared at her—but he'd stared at other people, too. Some people, especially a man described as strange, lacked the intuitive knowledge of social cues and boundaries.

Daniel couldn't forget that Glenn had been there

the day Lindsay got the call about Shane Ramsey collapsing after his uncle beat him. He hung around the office enough to know what was going on and remained friendly enough with the caseworkers he'd formerly supervised to hear about the child rape case that followed so soon after Martin Ramsey's murder.

Glenn had also proved to be remarkably hard to pin down. Nobody really knew whether he'd had hobbies back when he was still working. Because he hadn't talked about any, the consensus was that he lived for his job. If that was so, the puzzling part was that he had chosen to retire sooner than he had to.

Unless, of course, he'd decided it was time to start hunting the worst abusers in a more satisfying way than slapping them with too-short prison terms.

The two men were a contrast in that Glenn was helpful whenever Daniel called, while Zeller had yet to answer a call from Daniel or answer the door when he made follow-up visits. Ross Zeller's behavior should be more suspicious…but a serial killer who hadn't yet made a mistake might well be an Oscar-worthy actor.

After clearing the dishes that evening, Lindsay sat down again at the table, not happy to see that Daniel was already on his second cup of coffee, and said, "That'll keep you awake."

He smiled crookedly. "That's the general idea."

"You can't—"

"I can."

Refusing to back down, she suggested, "Why don't

I keep watch for a few hours tonight so you can really sleep? I can take a nap tomorrow."

"You can't leave the house."

"Is that necessary, if I make your usual rounds inside?"

"You have no experience with patrolling, sentry duty, being a bodyguard," he said flatly.

She crossed her arms and held his stare. "I have good eyesight, and I'm highly motivated. What else is required?"

"This is my job."

Absorbing that, she hid how much it hurt. As calmly as she could manage, she said, "Well, that puts me in my place. If you'll excuse me, I think I'll go read for a while. That'll give you peace and quiet to mainline your caffeine." She stood and started toward the doorway.

Behind her, a chair scraped across the polished wood floor. "Damn it, Lindsay, I didn't mean it the way you're thinking."

She paused briefly, closing her eyes. Why had she said that? She was hugely in debt to Daniel. Yes, they were sleeping together, but that didn't mean he was thinking of her as part of his future beyond nailing a killer. The last thing she should do was add any awkwardness to the relationship when they couldn't avoid each other.

She flapped a hand. "Forget about it. I'm irritated that you won't let me help, that's all."

"Would you turn around?" His voice came out huskier than usual.

Lindsay swallowed, took a few deep breaths and summoned her inner actress before she faced him.

Even more lines had deepened in his face. *"You're* not a job to me. You have to know that."

"Sure." She smiled. "I didn't mean to start something. Don't worry about it."

"I will worry about it." He held out a hand.

Barely hesitating, she reached out. His much larger hand engulfed hers, and he tugged her toward him.

"I've been trying to focus on keeping you safe," he said in that almost gruff voice. "I figured the rest could wait."

"It can," she whispered.

"I've never brought anyone involved in one of my investigations home with me."

Lindsay nodded. She'd assumed as much.

"You're depending on me right now. Putting pressure on you would be a crappy thing to do. Just know that the idea of something happening to you—" He swallowed. Shuddered, if she wasn't mistaken. "I don't know how I could live with that."

The melting sensation inside her rib cage made her eyes sting, too. "I'm not very good at saying thank you. If not for you—"

He cut her off. "Damn it, you're not listening! Gratitude is the last thing I want from you."

"I've been afraid of assuming anything," she said honestly. "So…maybe it's better if we hold off on this conversation."

"We can do that, but you need to know that you're not an obligation to me. You're…important."

Her head bobbed. "You're important to me, too. I—" *No, don't say it.* Instead, she changed gears. "I want the right to worry about you, too, though."

He bent down until his forehead rested against hers. "You can do that," he murmured. "I've been doing plenty of worrying about you."

He wouldn't be able to see her mouth, but she summoned a shaky smile anyway. "I know."

The next moment, he was kissing her. The passion and raw need ignited a response from her as powerful as his. The kiss went on and on as she did her best to mold her body to his, to tell him without words how she really felt.

Suddenly, though, he lifted his head and looked down at her. "You're right, and I was wrong," he said, sounding as if somebody had taken sandpaper to his vocal cords.

Lindsay blinked. How was she right?

"I need you now, but after that I also need some sleep. As long as you promise to wake me up if anything at all catches your attention."

Despite his dominant personality and strong, protective instincts, he was backing down. He intended to trust her enough to allow himself to sink into a deep sleep.

She gave him a smile. "Those are magic words, you know. I should have them tattooed where I can see them forever."

Showing a hint of wariness, he cocked his head. "Which words?"

"'You're right, and I was wrong.' What else?"

Seeing her full-fledged grin, he laughed. "Later I may have to deny I ever said that."

"Just try it."

His mouth still curved, he kissed her again. This time, he steered her toward the stairs.

IN THE NEXT few days, boredom took a toll on Lindsay. She'd never been sick or injured enough to be confined to her house for any length of time. Vacations? Who had time for those? And on the rare occasion when she'd managed to take one, she didn't use it to huddle inside.

Here, even when she walked around inside the house, she had to avoid passing in front of a window. She loved to read—but not all day long, every day. She'd taken to baking ridiculous quantities of breads, cookies, cakes and pies. The other cops who took turns guarding her took some of the bounty home. Daniel took some to work, too, but he didn't want other cops and employees to start wondering where he was coming by so many obviously home-baked goodies. Bread and cookies she put in the freezer. Whether she was here down the line or not, Daniel wouldn't lack for desserts.

She browsed job openings on the internet, and the reputations of local contractors, just in case she decided to rebuild her house. She looked up blueprints and designs—if she did build, she might as well improve on the basic rambler she'd bought when she'd first moved to Sadler.

She studied the latest model cars. She ordered a

dozen new books from an online bookseller. Clothes, too. Daniel wasn't thrilled to learn how often the UPS or FedEx truck rumbled up the driveway to his house, but the packages all came in his name and he scrawled notes to stick to the door permitting the drivers to leave everything on the porch.

"I've turned into a shopaholic," she told Melinda as she ripped open a shoebox. She was pretty sure these would fit. Even so, when she took out the riding boots, she made a face. "As if I'll ever get to ride again."

Melinda laughed at her. "Gloom and doom. Hey, don't forget the bright side. You're alive and you have a sexy boyfriend."

"Those are definitely silver linings," Lindsay admitted. She wouldn't have said anything to the woman detective about her relationship with Daniel, but he'd taken to kissing her when he got home, right in front of Melinda or Tom Alvarez or the couple of other cops who'd become her best—and only—friends.

Not true. She still had her phone, and Glenn and Sadie, at least, hadn't forgotten her. Most of the rest of her coworkers quit calling, no surprise when she couldn't meet up for coffee, had no idea what was happening at work and dodged any questions about where she was staying and when she'd be back.

Pursuing her earlier thought, though, she said, "Poor Daniel doesn't get to ride, either. Even if he had time, he'd feel bad abandoning me." He did still have to feed his animals and check on them, but probably astonished them with his haste.

"The horses don't look like they're in mourning."

Melinda was right in front of the kitchen window, where she could see the pasture.

"I know that's true." Lindsay kicked off her flip-flops and tried on the boots. They were amazingly comfortable, thank goodness. She lifted a foot, admiring the glossy black boot. "I'll look good when I do get paroled."

Melinda laughed at her again and talked her out of making another batch of cookies.

THREE TENSE DAYS LATER, Lindsay was clinging to Melinda's reminders of what she had to be thankful for as if it were a talisman holding magical properties. Face drawn, Daniel had less and less to say. She didn't have anything to say, either. She kept wondering how long his cop friends would be willing to give up their days off for a woman they hadn't even known before all this started. She kept wondering when the next body would be found…and who it would be.

Most often, she and Daniel made love before she got dressed again and began the assigned rounds he'd agreed to making routine. There was an increasing desperation to the way they clutched each other, a silent intensity to every touch.

Tonight, as she went downstairs in the dark, Lindsay was ruefully conscious of how well used her body felt and how relaxed. It and her brain had a real disconnect right now. Although she would never tell Daniel, she was growing to hate these dark hours on her own. At each window, she stood still, eyes burning with the need to see even the tiniest movement or anomaly through the slit of the blinds. That shape behind the fence was too big for a horse… But then she saw a foal bounce toward her, and after that, she recognized the larger bulk of what was probably his dam.

Tonight the moon was only a sliver from full, which helped. When it became a crescent, how would they see anything?

She moved to the next window and the next. Was that a car engine she heard? Quivering, she listened, but it wasn't close by. People were out on the roads at night. It wasn't really even that late.

An hour later, she'd circled the house again several times, sometimes seeing mirages that faded away when she looked hard enough. Once she saw what she first thought was a dog trotting across an open stretch of land before realizing it had to be a coyote. Were coyotes a threat to foals? She watched until it vanished from sight.

With a sigh, she wandered down the hall toward the open living space. The kitchen seemed…bright. Puzzled, her inner alarms flaring, she reminded herself there were lit numbers on the stove and microwave. Only none of those lights were orange.

Lindsay ran the last few steps, where the window framed a hot orange light. Fire.

"Daniel!" she screamed.

Chapter Fifteen

Daniel's feet hit the floor before he was fully awake. He grabbed the pants he'd left draped on a chair and yanked them on, pulled on a Kevlar vest over his bare torso and shoved sockless feet into boots. Gun in his right hand, fumbling to close the Velcro strips on the vest, he ran for the stairs.

She waited for him at the bottom. "The house is on fire! I don't know how it happened so fast. I looked out the kitchen window not that long ago, and now flames are climbing the wall. We can't go out that way."

"Have you called—"

"Yes." Stress thinned her voice, but she held on to outward calm. "What can we do?"

"I'm going to arrest this excuse for a human being," he snapped.

She wrung her hands. "What if he's waiting?"

"I'm counting on it," he said grimly.

"How…how will you get out?"

A shrill scream hurt his ear drums. Fire alarm,

which meant that in seconds… With a hiss, sprinklers came on.

He had to shout with his mouth at Lindsay's ear. "A window. Come with me."

He hustled her to his office in the corner on the opposite side of the house from the kitchen. There, he slid the wood-framed window open and shoved out the screen. He was already wet and saw that her hair hung in dripping hanks.

"Do you have the gun?" he asked.

He couldn't hear her answer, but she nodded and reached to retrieve it from the waistband at her lower back.

Holding her close, he put his mouth close to her ear. "Stay here unless it looks like the fire will trap you. Okay?"

"What if he gets in the house?"

"Shoot him." Daniel's hands tightened on her shoulders as he fought the need to stay with her. His best chance of catching this monster at last was to hunt him down outside.

He looked out, seeing nobody, before he planted a hand on the sill and vaulted out the window. A shrill neigh carried from the pasture, then another. What if the fire roared across the dry grass to surround his horses?

Daniel gritted his teeth.

Instinct had him trotting toward the back corner of his converted barn. The fire burned on the opposite side. It didn't seem likely the arsonist would be standing on the front porch. Unless he had already fled?

Daniel rejected that thought. This killer was here for Lindsay. Why would he leave now when he had them on the run?

Yeah, and where was his car?

Daniel flattened himself against the rough board siding, gun held in a two-handed grip and took a quick look around the corner. Damn. He didn't see anything but the horses cantering in panicked circles out in the pasture. The fire hadn't reached there, thank God.

Moving fast, he crossed the distance to the other back corner. He flattened himself there before fear crawled up his spine. Had he just behaved predictably? Leaving Lindsay alone in a room with an open window?

He mumbled some of the worst words he knew as he ran back the way he'd come.

LINDSAY BACKED INTO the closet after Daniel was gone. She'd be hard to spot here. If someone—say, a vicious killer—looked into the room without entering, he wouldn't see her.

The gun shook because her hands were trembling, but she held it ready to fire. She wished she could hear better, but the hiss of the sprinklers obscured any sound coming from outside. Would she even be able to hear sirens?

Please let help come fast, she begged silently.

Her vision kept blurring. She panted, blinking moisture from her eyes. When they opened, she saw a dark shape looming just outside the window. It might be Daniel…but if so, why wasn't he saying anything? And if it wasn't…

Just as the man started to climb in, awkwardly compared to Daniel's exit, she made out a dark, smooth covering on his head. And something covered most of his face.

Thoughts darted through her head as she pressed back in the open closet. Had he seen her? *Shoot him*, Daniel had said. But Lindsay had never imagined shooting a human being, or even an animal, with the intent of killing.

Staying silent, the figure paused with a leg over the sill.

"Stop!" she yelled, without having planned it.

"There you are."

At least, that's what she thought he said.

She shifted the barrel of the small handgun slightly to the side and pulled the trigger. *Bang!* Glass splintered.

He kept coming, not believing she would actually shoot him. Because he knew her. *Thought* he knew her.

Oh God, oh God. Lindsay pointed the gun at him and fired.

When he yelled, she discovered she'd closed her eyes when she pulled the trigger. She opened them just in time to see him fall back out the window. More gunshots sounded almost instantly.

Freaked, she crept toward the window even knowing Daniel wouldn't want her risking herself. But what if the killer had fired those shots and Daniel was down?

The first thing she saw was the man running away with a lurching gait. One leg didn't work right. Her shot might have hit his thigh.

She looked in the other direction and her breath caught. Daniel lay sprawled on the grass. Her heart stopped. But he wasn't dead, she realized in a second. He held his gun extended in both hands, and as she watched he fired it. The running man jerked as if he'd been hit but kept going.

Lindsay scrambled out the window, tumbling painfully to her hands and knees, but jumped up immediately and racing to Daniel.

"You're hurt!"

"Shoulder." He rolled and climbed to his feet. "Hell. I'm not letting him get away."

The moonlight let her see the blood spilling down his arm and over the Kevlar vest. Too much blood. Lindsay exclaimed, "You can't go after him."

"Watch me." He took two strides before stopping. "What am I thinking? We can head him off. You can't stay here alone."

She took that to mean she should follow him. He ran for the front of the house, never even turning his head toward the fire that illuminated the night so weirdly. He was intent on the garage. Reaching it, he tapped in a code on a keypad she hadn't even noticed was there and the door rose.

Sirens wailed in the distance, but he paid no more attention to those than he had the fire.

Within moments they were both in his truck. She thought the keys were surely in the house, but he took them from his pocket and started up the engine. He accelerated so fast her head snapped back.

"Can you see him?" he asked.

She searched the open ground. "No. But he could turn around once he knows we're gone."

"Why would he?"

"If he thinks you left me…" Because *she* was the target. She couldn't forget that.

"He stopped to see what we were going to do. He knows you're with me." Daniel's voice was gravel-rough. "He'll have heard the sirens, too. He's running."

The truck swayed as they rocketed toward the road.

DANIEL FOUGHT FOR control as he pushed his pickup to an unsafe speed. His arm would hurt like hell later, but right now it was numb. He could feel the weakness in it, though, and damned if it wasn't his right side. He couldn't believe he'd let that scumsucker wound him. In his fear for Lindsay, he'd come around the corner of the house too fast, incautiously. His own shots had hit the bastard's center mass, he'd swear they had, which must mean the killer wore a vest, too. Of course he did, Daniel thought in disgust. He'd planned for any eventuality before each murder, hadn't he? If he got away this time—

Daniel savagely pulled himself back to the here

and now. He'd be at the road in seconds and have to make a decision.

"I heard a car not that long ago," Lindsay said suddenly.

He chanced a quick look at her to see that she gripped her seat belt in one hand, the armrest with the other. She sat so stiffly, her back didn't touch the seat.

"Could you tell where?" he asked.

"I can't be sure, but I think it was right." She had to be terrified, but she hadn't so much as whimpered.

"Smartest place for him to leave the car."

He did brake, but they were still moving fast when he swerved onto the paved two-lane road. The pickup truck rocked and tires squealed as he laid down rubber. Pain finally stabbed his shoulder and upper arm, but it wasn't so bad he couldn't ignore it. As he accelerated again, he saw the flashing lights of an approaching fire truck in his rearview mirror.

Using his injured arm, he reached for his phone. Patted the pocket, then the one on the other side.

He mumbled a profanity. "Lost my phone." And, damn, trying to lift his hand back to the wheel awakened a new bolt of pain. His hand and arm weren't following orders, either. He dismissed thoughts of nerve damage. Like so much else, they could wait.

Impatiently, he asked, "Can you call Melinda or Alvarez?"

She produced her phone and dialed. When a voice answered, she put the call on speaker.

He updated Melinda in a few words and asked her to get as many officers as were immediately available to blockade this corner of the county. "Don't know what he's driving, but I'm betting on the white sedan."

"On my way."

"Wait, are you still there? This guy's got a gun and he's wearing Kevlar. He won't hesitate to shoot."

Some corner of his attention noted that his right hand was covered in blood. He was probably dripping onto the upholstery, too.

A deer appeared in the headlights, leaping a ditch and disappearing before Daniel had to brake. First movement he'd seen.

Maybe he should slow down. What if he passed that white Corolla, tucked out of sight off the road? That piece of scum could wait until the sound of his engine receded, pull out and sedately drive home. Nice to think he'd be spotted by another officer, but in reality there would be only one or two patrolling at this time of night, and they could well be on the other side of town or even responding to a call. Chaney wouldn't do them any more good; at night, his department probably had only one deputy covering the entire county.

Daniel's foot eased up on the accelerator and the speed dropped. At least he had two sets of eyes. At the moment, he trusted Lindsay's more than his own. The pain, or maybe the blood loss, was getting to him.

If this monster escaped to kill again, Daniel might not be able to forgive himself.

"I see something," Lindsay said suddenly.

"What—" Red taillights appeared ahead. Low to

the ground. A car, and not a big one. Plus, these had to be on an older model.

Daniel slammed the gas pedal to the floor. With V8 at his control, the truck charged forward. If he thought he could safely run in the dark, he would have. As it was, he saw that the car ahead of him had immediately accelerated, too. Any other car on the road would have maintained a steady speed, or even pulled over when the driver became aware of a larger vehicle bearing down on him at high speed.

Still Lindsay didn't say a word, although he was distantly aware that her body was completely rigid. She knew what was at stake here. She'd been courageous during events far outside her experience.

They were closing in. Near enough to see the car ahead was white, and so small he damn well could run right over it.

"What are you going to do?" she asked, her voice thin.

"Run him off the road." Later he'd be irked that he'd had to damage his own truck, but that wasn't even a consideration right now. He was more worried about what would happen once both vehicles came to a standstill. This wasn't a man who'd put his hands in the air and surrender. Daniel didn't even know if he'd prefer that. A part of him regretted Lindsay's presence, because the knowledge that she was watching would keep him from stepping over the line.

The sedan began to weave from one side of the road to the other in an attempt to keep him from pulling alongside.

"Hold on," Daniel warned, and tapped the other vehicle's bumper. Metal screeched. A small gasp was the only giveaway of Lindsay's tension.

The Corolla kept swerving, but erratically now, as though the driver had lost control. Daniel chose his moment and sped up again, this time scraping his fender alongside the smaller car's. Then he yanked the wheel to the right, and the Corolla flew off the road into a barbed wire fence that worked like an arresting wire on an aircraft carrier deck.

Fighting to keep the truck on the road, Daniel braked hard, but it took time to stop. The minute he did, he threw the gear into Reverse and sped backward.

"Get down," he ordered. "He might come out shooting."

She unsnapped her seat belt and slid to her knees on the floorboard. In a matter of seconds, he braked with the pickup slightly behind the sedan. Then he threw open his door and jumped out, bending over to take advantage of the protection the metal body of his Ford offered.

He pulled his Glock from his lower back but found he couldn't lift it with his right hand. Damn. He had a familiar sensation of time having slowed, as if the scene clicked forward like old-fashioned slides.

The car's driver wasn't moving. He seemed to be slumped forward. With luck his head had slammed into the windshield, but Daniel didn't buy it. Moonlight let him see that the glass hadn't cracked into the telltale spiderweb pattern. Weapon held out in a two-hand grip, his left hand bearing most of the weight, he jumped the ditch and advanced on the tilted white car.

"Police!" he yelled. "Put your hands on your head! Let me see them."

The man didn't move.

Hip against the fender and then the back door, Daniel stayed behind the driver, watching for any giveaways. When he reached the driver door, he had to brace his right hand against the glass of the passenger side back window to free his left hand to wrench open the door.

Not locked, was the last thing he thought before the man now only inches away exploded into motion.

LINDSAY HAD CALLED Melinda even before Daniel jumped out of the truck. She couldn't tell if he even heard her.

"The attacker was wounded, and he ran. Daniel and I pursued in his pickup truck. When we saw an older Toyota Corolla, it sped up. Daniel ran it off the road and he's approaching the driver door now." She named the road and gave Melinda her best guess of how far they'd driven, then ended the call without waiting for a response. She had to see what was happening.

She took out her own gun again, as alien as it felt in her hands, and cautiously raised her head to see Daniel's broad back. He was opening the sedan's driver door with one hand…when the killer twisted in his seat and a gun barked.

Daniel reeled back. Then, shot again or not, he

lunged forward and wrapped his arms around the other man and yanked him out of the car.

By that time, Lindsay had jumped out and was scrambling toward the two men wrestling for control. Daniel was the bigger, the more powerful, she saw immediately, but his right arm hung at his side and his gun had disappeared. Had it fallen from his hand?

The truck headlights partially illuminated the scene, just as the car's headlights speared the darkness of what might be a pasture.

Daniel spun his adversary and used his weight and strength to pin him against the back door. But, on a spurt of terror, Lindsay saw the pistol still clutched in the other man's hand. He was struggling to turn it. He couldn't see her approaching, so she got within feet of the two men and cried, "Drop the gun or I'll shoot!"

The barrel swung toward her. She couldn't see most of him, but his arm would do. This close, she couldn't miss. Grimly willing her eyes to stay open, she aimed and squeezed the trigger. As she heard the scream, the gun dropped from his hand.

"I'm kicking his gun under the car," she told Daniel, sounding astonishingly collected.

With what had to be a massive effort, he spun the killer and slammed him face-first against the metal of the car.

"I have cuffs in the glove compartment." Daniel's voice was guttural.

She put the safety on her borrowed gun and tucked it back in her waistband, then made her way back up the bank to the truck. Within moments, she returned.

"I have them."

"Snap one cuff on this wrist." Daniel pulled the man's right hand back despite another agonized scream.

The cuffs were metal ones, thank goodness; she didn't even know how the plastic ones worked. But she closed first one cuff on the wrist Daniel forced into view, then the second.

In moments, the man who'd tried to burn them out of Daniel's house tonight and killed so many people lay facedown on the ground. Daniel drilled one knee between his shoulder blades. "You're under arrest. You have the right to remain silent. Anything you say can and will be used against you in a court of law."

He went on, every word in that same raw, angry voice. Not until he finished did he raise his head.

His expression was nothing Lindsay had ever seen or ever wanted to see again. And yet, for all the rage there, he'd continued to do his job. He would have died to stop this man, both because of the atrocities he'd committed and to keep her safe. Her heart squeezed with love too painful to give joy.

Only then did she lower her gaze to the now diminished man who kept his head turned away from her. She circled behind Daniel, around the feet wearing white athletic shoes stained with blood, until she saw the face.

She wanted to be surprised, but couldn't.

"How could you do such terrible things?" she asked her mentor, her friend.

"I'd have done anything for you." Bitterness corroded his low voice. Without trying to meet her eyes, Glenn turned his head away.

She pressed her hand against her stomach to try to contain the nausea. He'd tortured and killed for her. What had she ever done or said to make him think she'd want any such thing?

She suddenly realized that Daniel was looking at her. Despite his pain and the banked anger, what his eyes held was understanding.

"It was never about you."

She managed a nod and backed away just as a police car screamed to a stop right behind Daniel's truck.

Epilogue

Every time Daniel surfaced from the anesthesia-induced grogginess, he asked for Lindsay. If he got answers, he didn't remember them the next time he awakened.

This time, he opened his eyes, worked his mouth and understood from the curtains pulled around the bed that he was in the hospital and no longer in recovery.

"Lindsay," he mumbled.

Like an angel, she appeared beside the bed. "You're awake." She gave him some sips of water and slivers of ice to roll around in his mouth.

"You're here," he managed. Brilliant.

"Because you kept asking for me." She smiled. "Otherwise they might not have let me in because I'm not family."

He groaned. His family would descend on the hospital room like a plague of locusts once they heard he'd been injured again.

"Melinda called and spoke to your mother. They'll be here in the next hour or two."

He reached across his body with his left hand and seized her wrist. "Don't leave."

She sat on the edge of the bed. "I don't know if I'll be allowed to stay."

"Fiancée."

Her eyes widened. "What?"

He repeated himself.

"I'm…not a very good liar."

"No lie." He worked his mouth until he could speak a little more coherently. "Doesn't have to be."

"You're asking…"

"Please." He took a deep breath that hinted at on-coming pain. "We don't have to hurry, but I don't want you to move out."

"Oh." She nibbled on her lip. "You know your house suffered some damage?"

He hadn't given his house a thought yet. And, damn, then there was his truck. "Bad?"

"According to the fire chief, no. A good part of one wall will need to be replaced, the kitchen door, and some work on the eaves. But with the sprinklers, the fire didn't progress, even fueled by gasoline."

"Good." He ought to release her but didn't want to. "You know what they did to me?"

What she told him rang a bell. The nurse in re-covery had probably said the same. The surgeon had removed a bullet from his shoulder, and he had bro-ken ribs from the two bullets that had struck his Kev-lar vest.

He looked down at his right hand. The response was sluggish when he commanded it to ball into a fist, but eventually he managed it. He closed his eyes briefly in relief.

A hand cupped his jaw. "You'll have to do some physical therapy to get back full function, but the surgeon is confident that if you do your part, it will happen."

"Good." His jaw was probably scratching the palm of her hand, but he let go of her wrist to lay his left hand atop hers, pressing it to his cheek. He turned his head enough to kiss her palm. Daniel couldn't help noticing she hadn't given him an answer on the marriage/living together question. Or had he actually asked?

Probably not, he decided. He tried again. "Will you stay with me?"

"Here? Or…after they let you go home?"

"Both."

This time, she didn't look away. "The idea is scary for me. You know that. But… I loved living with you. I want to do that. To find out if we both keep feeling the same. So…yes."

"Love you," he whispered.

Lindsay bent forward to touch her forehead to his. "I love you, too."

"You can trust me."

As if startled, she straightened up, searching his eyes. "I know that! How can you think…" And then emotions crossed her face too quickly for him to identify, although bewilderment was in there somewhere. At the end came an unfamiliar softness. "Of course

I trust you. You would have given everything to protect me, wouldn't you?"

If by everything, she meant his life, the answer was yes.

A smile bloomed slowly on her face, making him think of dawn. But all she said was, "They'll have to drag me out of here kicking and screaming."

That constituted all the promise he needed. He wrapped his working hand around her nape and drew her down again, until he felt her breath on his neck.

Then he fell asleep again.

* * * * *

#1929 AMBUSH BEFORE SUNRISE
Cardwell Ranch: Montana Legacy • by B.J. Daniels
Wrangler Angus Savage has come to Wyoming to reconnect with
Jinx McCallahan and help her get her cattle to high country. But when they
set out on the trail, they don't expect to come across so many hazards—
including Jinx's treacherous ex, who wants her back...or dead.

#1930 MIDNIGHT ABDUCTION
Tactical Crime Division • by Nichole Severn
When Benning Reeves's twins are kidnapped, the frantic father asks
Ana Ramirez and the Tactical Crime Division of the FBI for help. As evidence
accumulates, they'll have to discover why this situation connects to an
unresolved case...before it's too late.

#1931 EVASIVE ACTION
Holding the Line • by Carol Ericson
Minutes before her wedding, April Hart learns her fiancé is a drug lord. Now
the only person she can trust is a man from her past—border patrol agent
Clay Archer. April left Clay to protect him from her dangerous family, so this
time Clay is determined to guard April—and his heart.

#1932 WHAT SHE SAW
Rushing Creek Crime Spree • by Barb Han
Deputy Courtney Foster's brief fling with Texas ranch owner Jordan Kent
was her time-out after getting shot in the line of duty. Only now she's
hunting a killer...and she just discovered she's pregnant.

#1933 ISOLATED THREAT
A Badlands Cops Novel • by Nicole Helm
When Cecilia Mills asks sheriff's deputy Brady Wyatt to help her hide a child
from his father's biker gang, Brady will put his life on the line to keep all
three of them safe from the Sons of the Badlands.

#1934 WITHOUT A TRACE
An Echo Lake Novel • by Amanda Stevens
When Rae Cavanaugh's niece mysteriously goes missing, county sheriff
Tom Brannon is determined to find her. But as electricity sparks between
Rae and Tom, Rae discovers—despite her misgivings—Tom is the only one
she can trust...

Prologue

They warned him not to go to the police.

He couldn't think. Couldn't breathe.

Forcing one foot in front of the other, he tried to ignore the gut-wrenching pain at the base of his skull where the kidnapper had slammed him into his kitchen floor and knocked him unconscious. Owen. Olivia. They were out there. Alone. Scared. He hadn't been strong enough to protect them, but he wasn't going to stop trying to find them. Not until he got them back.

A wave of dizziness tilted the world on its axis, and he collided with a wooden street pole. Shoulder-length hair blocked his vision as he fought to regain balance. He'd woken up a little less than fifteen minutes ago, started chasing after the taillights of the SUV as it'd sped down the unpaved road leading into town. He could still taste the dirt in his mouth. They couldn't have gotten far. Someone had to have seen something…

Humidity settled deep into his lungs despite the dropping temperatures, sweat beading at his temples as he pushed himself upright. Moonlight beamed down on him, exhaustion pulling at every muscle in his body, but he had to keep going. He had to find his kids. They were all he had left. All that mattered.

Colorless worn mom-and-pop stores lining the town's main street blurred in his vision.

A small group of teenagers—at least what looked like teenagers—gathered around a single point on the sidewalk ahead. The kidnapper had sped into town from his property just on the outskirts, and there were only so many roads that would get the bastard out. Maybe someone in the group could point him in the right direction. He latched on to a kid brushing past him by the collar. "Did you see a black SUV speed through here?"

The boy—sixteen, seventeen—shook his head and pulled away. "Get off me, man."

The echo of voices pierced through the ringing in his ears as the circle of teens closed in on itself in front of Sevierville's oldest hardware store. His lungs burned with shallow breaths as he searched the streets from his position in the middle of the sidewalk. Someone had to have seen something. Anything. He needed—

"She's bleeding!" a girl said. "Someone call for an ambulance!"

The hairs on the back of his neck stood on end. Someone had been hurt? Pushing through the circle of onlookers, he caught sight of pink pajama pants and bright purple toenails. He surrendered to the panic as recognition flared. His heart threatened to burst straight out of his chest as he lunged for the unconscious six-year-old girl sprawled across the pavement. Pain shot through his knees as he scooped her into his arms. "Olivia!"

Don't miss
Midnight Abduction *by Nichole Severn,*
available June 2020 wherever
Harlequin Intrigue books and ebooks are sold.

Harlequin.com

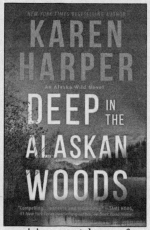

Love Harlequin romance?

DISCOVER.

Be the first to find out about promotions,
news and exclusive content!

 Facebook.com/HarlequinBooks

 Twitter.com/HarlequinBooks

 Instagram.com/HarlequinBooks

 Pinterest.com/HarlequinBooks

 ReaderService.com

EXPLORE.

Sign up for the Harlequin e-newsletter and
download a free book from any series at
TryHarlequin.com

CONNECT.

Join our Harlequin community to
share your thoughts and connect
with other romance readers!
Facebook.com/groups/HarlequinConnection

HSOCIAL2020